"Marriage!"
The Word Rang Out Again
Before She Could Hold It Back.

But who could blame her? Last morning, she'd woken up never expecting to see Rashid again. This morning, she woke up in his bed.

"Of course. I took your innocence."

"You didn't 'take my innocence,' I gave it to you. And will you stop being so archaic and so—so… Azmaharian?"

"You're refusing to marry me?"

Her heartstrings shook at the darkness in his rumble. "I'm refusing to introduce the concept of 'marriage' at this point."

And if displeasure could take form, it would wear just that face. "Marriage between us now is not a concept, it's a necessity."

Dear Reader,

When Rashid Aal Munsoori walked into the Desert Knights trilogy's first book, *The Sheikh's Redemption,* and hijacked the spotlight during his scenes, he intrigued me the most of all my Harlequin Desire heroes to date. With each glimpse he revealed of himself, I knew I had my darkest, most tormented, most ruthless Desire hero yet. I couldn't wait for him to tell me his whole story. And for a heroine to undertake the seemingly impossible task of soothing this scarred beast and laying his demons to rest.

But I knew I had my work cut out for me. For what woman could see through his armor of disfigurement and distance, let alone persevere until she'd uncovered the passionate, forever-man he could be?

Then I discovered I had already created that heroine. Laylah Aal Shalaan had appeared in *To Tame a Sheikh,* the first book of my previous trilogy, Pride of Zohayd. And she told me she'd loved Rashid all her life. Did *that* turn the unapproachable Rashid inside out!

What followed was a roller coaster of emotions as Laylah unraveled the bonds around Rashid's soul and replaced them with those of her love, only to discover at her happiest that their relationship had all been a lie. Or was it?

Read on and learn the truth behind the secrets that wrap up *Desert Knights* among the upheavals that the lovers have to survive to reach their happy ending. I hope you enjoy reading their story as much as I did writing it.

I love to hear from readers, so email me at oliviagates@gmail.com. And please stay connected with me on Facebook at my fan page Olivia Gates Author, and on Twitter @OliviaGates.

Thanks for reading!

Olivia

OLIVIA GATES

THE SHEIKH'S DESTINY

HARLEQUIN®

entertain, enrich, inspire™

Recycling programs
for this product may
not exist in your area.

ISBN-13: 978-0-373-73214-2

THE SHEIKH'S DESTINY

www.Harlequin.com

Printed in U.S.A.

Books by Olivia Gates

Harlequin Desire

Silhouette Desire

Other titles by this author available in ebook format.

OLIVIA GATES

has always pursued creative passions such as singing and handicrafts. She still does, but only one of her passions grew gratifying enough, consuming enough, to become an ongoing career—writing.

She is most fulfilled when she is creating worlds and conflicts for her characters, then exploring and untangling them bit by bit, sharing her protagonists' every heart-wrenching heart-ache and hope, their every heart-pounding doubt and trial, until she leads them to an indisputably earned and gloriously satisfying happy ending.

When she's not writing, she is a doctor, a wife to her own alpha male and a mother to one brilliant girl and one demanding Angora cat. Visit Olivia at www.oliviagates.com.

To the one who inspires all those
powerful, ultra-romantic, luscious heroes.
Thank you for being you.

One

Laylah Aal Shalaan felt a shiver burn down her spine.

It wasn't the below-zero Chicago December evening. That would have caused ice, not fire, to shudder through her veins.

This sensation had scalded through her so many times during the past few weeks, it was as if she were having hot flashes. Which would be some record at age twenty-seven. But then she held other unwelcome records. Like being the only female born to her family in forty years. Why not throw in premature menopause, too?

Not that she really thought abnormal hormones were at work here. An outside influence was. One she couldn't detect when she'd tried to investigate it, though she'd been certain of its cause for some time.

Someone was watching her.

This felt nothing like having the security detail she'd once had breathing down her neck. Those men had never tried to hide themselves, and to hell with her personal space. Though she shouldn't have resented them. They'd been doing their job. Of course, with her safety no longer among anyone's priorities for the past two years, there were no more guards dogging her steps.

Not that she thought that she needed protection. She observed normal safety protocols, like anyone who lived in Chicago did. And since she'd exiled herself from Zohayd and come to live in the Windy City, she always had.

Until tonight.

Usually she would go home with Mira, her business partner and roommate. But Mira had left to see her father, who had been taken to the E.R. in another state. So here she was, alone at night for the first time in more than two years, leaving the deserted building from the back exit that opened onto an equally empty back street.

Not that *that* had anything to do with what she now felt.

She'd entered the building accompanied by the sensation of being enveloped in that watchful force field. She'd stepped out only to be caught in its electrifying embrace again.

Strangest part was, she didn't feel threatened by that unwavering intent. Just burning with curiosity and…excitement?

She looked across the street at three parked cars. The nearest had a man slamming the hood, getting inside and driving away with the exhaust firing. The next one, also nondescript, was pulling away from the curb, too. The farthest one, a late-model Mercedes with dark windows, looked empty.

Before she could decide where the influence was radiating from, the second car suddenly floored its engine.

Before she could draw another breath, the car screeched to a halt beside her and its doors burst open. Four men exploded out. She'd barely taken two running steps when they swarmed her.

Hulking bodies and coarse faces, distorted with vile intent, filled her vision. Blood and time thickened, hindering her heartbeat and reactions as hands sank into her flesh, each dig creating a bolt of outrage and terror.

Dread exploded in her chest, fury in her skull as she lashed out with everything she had, even as shards of dialogue lodged into her brain.

"Iz only one, man."

"Tom said there'd be two. You better not pay half now."

"Iz the one we want. Ye'll get yer dough."

"You said she'd fall at 'ur feet sniveling but she ain't no push-over. She almost kneed me."

"An' she might've scratched m'eye out!"

"*You* quit snivelin' an' stuff 'er in the car."

Each word sank a talon of realization into Laylah's brain. This wasn't a random attack. They knew her routine.

No. They couldn't be the presence she'd been sensing!

They dragged her closer to the car. Once they shoved her inside, it would be over.

She exploded in another manic struggle, drawing blood and shouts of pain and rage until a jackhammer collided with her jaw. Agony turned her brain into shrapnel.

Suddenly, through the vortex of crimson-blotched darkness, one of her attackers seemed to be sucked away as if into a black hole. He slammed into the side of the building with a sickening crunch.

A second assailant turned away, but a hair-raising crack sent his blood arcing inches from her face. His terrified gaze bored into hers before his body slammed into her as if from the impact of a speeding car. He took her down with him.

She struggled under his dead weight, fear pulsing through her disorientation. Who had come to her rescue? Would they turn on her once they had finished off her attackers?

The body pinning her down was heaved away. She wriggled up frantically on the freezing sidewalk and saw...saw...

Him.

A fallen angel. Huge, dark, ominous. Frightening in his beauty, radiating power and menace. Almost impossible to bear looking at, yet equally impossible to look away from.

And she knew him. She'd known him all her life.

But it couldn't be him. Not only had he changed almost beyond recognition, but what would he be doing here? Now? When she'd been certain she'd never see him again?

Was her jolted brain conjuring up an imaginary savior?

If so, why not one of her cousins who were as well equipped to fill the role? Why him?

Why Rashid Aal Munsoori?

But with her senses stabilizing, no doubt remained. It *was* Rashid. A remote, if steady, presence in her life during her first seventeen years. The man she'd had a crush on since before she could remember.

He was now facing the remaining two attackers like a monolith, his one-of-a-kind face carved from the coldness of the night, majestic head almost shaved, juggernaut body swathed in a coat that flapped around him like angry creatures from the abyss.

The men recovered from their shock, charged him, snarling, slashing switchblades at him. Dread deluged her.

Unfazed by her shout or their attack, Rashid maneuvered like a matador fielding raging bulls, harnessing the mindlessness of their charge against them. His arms and legs lashed out in a choreography of deadly precision, his methods merciless, flawless, as second nature as breathing was to her. He looked like an avenging demon reveling in vanquishing the loathsome quarry he lived to prey on.

By the time she pulled herself to her feet, Rashid had the two men plastered against the building. One had lost consciousness. The other hung in the air, feet kicking feebly.

Over the night's moaning wind, she heard rumbles issuing from Rashid. They didn't sound human.

For a crazy moment, she thought they might not be. That he did have some…entity inhabiting him, one that wouldn't be satisfied with anything less than taking those men's lives.

That conviction broke her paralysis. "You'll kill them!"

At her choking protest he turned his head and…*ya Ruhmaan.*

Merciful God—what had happened to him? He barely resembled the man she'd obsessed over all her life. The eerie blankness in his eyes, the serene viciousness baring his teeth. Like a beast in killing mode.

And that *scar*...

"And?"

She shuddered. His voice. It completed the impression. That some demon occupied him, had taken him over, was metamorphosing his body to suit its nature and needs, was using his voice to transmit its darkness and danger.

This man who'd once been Rashid was serious in his question. He had no compunction about killing in principle, and none at all about snuffing out the lives of the thugs he'd conquered.

There was no way to appeal to the mercy of this creature. He had none. Of that she was certain. She couldn't use fear of consequences, either. She was as sure he felt no fear of any sort. He seemed to feel nothing but violence and vengeance. It was as if he'd stepped in to punish the criminals, not to save her, the victim.

Only appealing to his logic remained.

"*And* there's no need." She could barely form words in her frozen, constricted throat. "You've already beaten them—to a pulp. None of them will be out of intensive care anytime soon."

"Putting them back together will be a gross waste of medical resources. I should spare society the cost of their continued existence." He turned his eyes to the man wriggling and whimpering in his hold. "Scum like this don't deserve to live."

She ventured closer, feeling as if she was interrupting a lion's kill. "A death sentence is over the top for their crime, don't you think?"

Still looking at the struggling man, Rashid said, "The ones they've committed so far, you mean. They would have probably ended up killing you—"

"No, man…" The man choked, terror flowing from his eyes. "We were only…goin' to hold 'er…for ransom. A bro recognized 'er for a princess…from one o' those filthy rich oil kingdoms…said we'd get…serious dough…for 'er. We weren't going to hurt 'er…*or* touch 'er…" he spluttered the qualification when Rashid squeezed his throat harder. "I…*swear*. Danny got carried away when she hit him…and you probably killed him for it…but I didn't do anything to her…don't kill me…*please*…"

In spite of everything, she pitied this flimsy creature in the body of a brute. He'd been reduced to blubbering in the grip of a force the likes of which he hadn't known existed.

The imbalance of power should have been in their favor, four hulks versed in violence. But Rashid had overpowered them like a superior feline would a pack of rats.

But it was as if he didn't even feel her there, had been debating with his inner demon the actions he should take, finding only approval from it.

She had one last shot before this situation passed the point of no return. Give him, and that demon, something to appease their merciless convictions.

She ventured a touch on his arm, flinched. Even through the layers of clothes, electricity arced from the steel cables he had for muscles to strike her to her toes.

She swallowed a lump of agitation. "Wouldn't you rather they live to suffer the consequences of their crimes? You've probably given them all some permanent disability."

When his dark gaze turned to her again, it felt as if he was seeing her for the first time, letting her and her words breach the barrier of his implacability.

Suddenly, he unclenched his hands. The men, both unconscious now, thudded to the ground like sacks of bricks.

Relief shuddered through her, the freezing air filling her lungs. Rashid had killed before. But it had been as a soldier in three wars. Here, it would have been different. And she couldn't have even those thugs' deaths on her conscience.

As he stood appraising his handiwork, she sensed his demon scratching at its containment to be let loose to finish its job. But Rashid seemed in control of their symbiosis again, back to being the ultramodern desert knight who had the world at his feet and everyone in it at his disposal.

He produced his cell phone, called the police then an ambulance. Then he turned to her. "Did they hurt you?"

At his question, she suddenly felt the imprint of their hands all over her arms and back. But the epicenter of pain was the left side of her jaw. Her hand flew to it instinctively.

He urged her below a streetlight. She stumbled at the feel of his hand on her arm, then again as he kicked one of the thugs in the head when he began to stir. The contrast between his violence with her attacker and his gentleness with her was staggering.

Once within the circle of light, his hand moved hers away from her face so he could examine it.

"Maybe I will kill them after all."

She almost flinched at his verdict, attempted to make light of it. "For a right hook?"

"That was the beginning of the abuse that would have left you scarred for life, if not physically then psychologically. They do deserve to die." She grabbed his arm as he moved, feeling she had as much chance of stopping him as she would a hurricane. His muscles eased beneath her frantic fingers. "Relax. I'll only make them wish I had killed them."

"How about you leave it to the law to deal with them?"

His hooded eyes grew heavier with disapproval. "You'd rather let them get away with it?"

"Certainly not. I just believe in appropriate punishment."

Those lethal eyes flared ebony fire. "What would be appropriate for abusing and kidnapping a woman, putting her through hell fearing for her life, before maybe ending it?"

She bit her lip at the terrible scenario that could have come to pass if not for him. "When you put it that way, a death sentence doesn't look too extreme. But that didn't happen."

"Only because I stopped them."

"And now we can't punish them for what could have been, only for what actually was."

"That's according to the law—here. Where I come from only *hadd'al herabah* is appropriate punishment for this heinous crime."

She shuddered again as she imagined the ancient punishment

sanctioned in their home region for those caught red-handed
in major crimes like this—amputating an arm and a leg from
opposing sides.

Deeming the subject closed, he turned to the fallen goons.
And she saw it. A glistening wetness below his coat.

Sick electricity forked through her as she grabbed his arm,
jerked him into the light. He pulled away from her frantic grip,
made her grasp him to restore her balance. Her hands sank into
the unmistakable warmth of blood.

She tore them away, looked down at her crimson-stained
palms before looking up at him in horror. "You're injured!"

His gaze moved from her upturned hands to his midriff before travelling up to hers. "It's nothing."

"Nothing?" she exclaimed. "You're *bleeding! Ya Ullah!*"

Something like…annoyance? Impatience? simmered in his
eyes. "It's just a scratch."

"A scratch? Your whole left side is drenched in blood."

"And?" There he went again with that *and* of his. "Are you
squeamish? I hope you won't faint."

"Squeamish?" she exclaimed. "It's you I'm worried about…"

Dread clogged her throat, more suffocating than anything
she'd felt on her own account. His nonchalance had to be shock.
His wound had to be severe to bleed that much, to not have registered its pain yet. Adrenaline and cold must be all that was
keeping him on his feet. By the time the ambulance arrived, it
might be too late…

Stem his bleeding. Buy him time.

Tearing her scarf from around her neck, she lunged at him,
pressing its creamy softness against the tear in his sweater.
He stiffened, his hands covering hers as if to push them away.

She threw her weight at him, pressing him back against the
side of the building, panting now. "We must apply pressure."

He stilled against her, stared down at her, his face a mask.
Was he on the verge of losing consciousness?

He undid her hands, replaced them with his. "I'll do it." She sensed that he would, not because he believed he needed it, but to keep her away. "You can go now."

Huh? He didn't only want her to stay away, but to *go* away?

She shook her head, hands smeared in his blood trembling. "I have to be here when the police arrive."

He reached for her hands, wiping them clean with the other end of the scarf. "I'll say they attacked me. Those lowlifes will welcome my adjustment. A jury will give them a lesser sentence for attacking me rather than you."

"But you wanted them to get the harshest punishment possible."

"Whatever sentence the law passes won't be that. I am bound by no such limitations, and I'll make sure they'll never think of doing this to anyone else ever again."

"You mean you want them to get off lightly so you can administer your own brand of justice…?" She threw her hands up in the air. "What are we talking about? You're *injured.* And I'm going nowhere but to the E.R. with you."

"Since I'm not going to the E.R., the only place you can go now is home." At her head shake, his voice hardened. "Take my car and drive a few blocks away. My guards will come to escort you back home. They'll come up with you to make sure the coast is clear and will stand guard until we make sure this abduction plan had no contingencies." When she didn't move or answer he exhaled forcibly. "Go *now,* before the police arrive. You've been through enough on those scums' account. Walk away and forget this ever happened."

"I can't and won't leave you. And you *will* go to the E.R. Is that your car?" She indicated the imposing Mercedes.

He nodded. "I stopped to send a file from my phone."

"And that's when you saw me being attacked."

He didn't nod again, his gaze growing incapacitating.

"Give me your keys." A formidably winged eyebrow told her what he thought of her demand. "I'm driving you to the E.R."

"As you pointed out, I can't leave the crime scene. The police will be here in minutes."

"They can take *our* statements at the E.R. You might succumb to hypothermia and shock in those minutes."

"I will succumb to nothing. I've had injuries a dozen times worse, endured them for *days* in conditions that make these pleasant in comparison."

She knew he wasn't exaggerating. She couldn't imagine what he'd endured in war, couldn't bear to think what kind of injury had given him that blood-curdling scar that slithered like an angry snake from his left eye down to his jaw, neck…and below.

Noticing her eyes on his scar, his lips compressed. "As you can see I've survived far worse. Don't concern yourself over this glorified paper cut."

Retorts fired in her mind, froze on her tongue. What did he think her? A selfish twit who'd grab the easy way out and run away?

But if he thought so, then… "You don't recognize me?"

That eyebrow rose again. "I need to know someone to come to their rescue?"

"That's not what I meant." She knew he'd defend to the death anyone in need of his superior powers. He'd once made a career of it as a warrior. He'd clearly never stopped being one.

He just as clearly hadn't recognized her.

Then he said, "Of course I recognized you. Just like the one who sent those goons did. You're more recognizable than you evidently think you are, Princess Laylah."

So he *did* recognize her. Which actually shouldn't have been a sure thing. There'd been far…less of her when he'd last seen her, and she'd been wearing glasses back then, too. He'd always made her feel he'd never *seen* her, the way he'd look through her, like he had everyone else. Even now, nothing in his demeanor indicated that he knew her. The reticent Rashid she'd known had become impenetrable.

"I saw you many times around the city before tonight."

Would this man stop surprising her? "Y-you did? Where?"

"I have offices in this building. You also frequent the restaurants I do."

He had been the presence she'd felt!

Now *that* made sense. As did the fact that he hadn't thought of acknowledging her until he'd been forced to, to save her life no less. She'd always known Rashid had been a far-fetched dream, but he'd become an impossible one after he'd turned from her closest cousins' best friend to their mortal enemy.

"You clearly don't recognize me," he added.

"I'd as soon not recognize myself, Sheikh Rashid."

Everything in him seemed to hit Pause. The wind, the whole world followed suit.

Okay. That *had* come out too…revealing. Another attack of what her mother called her "crassness affliction." She'd thought she had it under control, but it seemed she couldn't control her brash candor any more than her mother's family could their crooked ways.

So be it. She'd never be able to give him anything of equal value to what he'd given her tonight, so she'd at least give him the truth. He could do with it as he wished.

It appeared he was at a loss what to do with it. Her confession had clearly stunned him.

His response, when it finally came, was to pretend he hadn't heard it and to pursue his previous point. "Back my statement, that they attacked me and not you, and I will go to the E.R."

He was trying to spare her the postattack ordeal, from the investigations through to the trial.

Still… "I can't let you bear the burden of this mess."

Those daunting shoulders barely moved in dismissal. "In comparison to the messes I deal with daily, this is a breeze."

She'd bet. Rashid had created his IT development empire from scratch in record time. He must have dealt with endless obstacles and adversaries to remain at the top of such a cutthroat field. And it *would* be a mess for her, sabotaging the peaceful life and low profile she'd struggled to create since she'd left Zohayd.

"Okay." The tension gripping the night eased, until she added, "But only if you let me drive you to the E.R."

"You think I won't keep my word?"

"I think you'd keep your word even if it meant your life."

Another long, empty stare greeted her statement, which she now realized signified surprise. "Why this stipulation, then? You think I can't drive myself?"

It was her turn to shrug. "I'm taking no chances."

His grimness deepened until she was certain he'd say no.

Suddenly, he handed her the bloody scarf. She fumbled with it as if with a hot coal as he fished inside his coat for a pen and a notebook. He scribbled a few lines, tore the paper out, bent and tucked it onto a thug. A calling card on gifts for the police?

The thug stirred as Rashid whispered in his ear before slamming him into the ground, snuffing his consciousness again.

Calmly rising, he retrieved the scarf from her limp fingers, turned on his heels and crossed the street to his car.

He was leaving?

She watched him go, at a loss for what to do.

Instead of taking the wheel, he walked around to the passenger's side. Then, leaning over the car's top, he looked across the distance at her. "Coming?"

Her heart gave a thunderclap of relief as she stumbled into a run, her four-inch stilettos a staccato of eagerness on the asphalt.

In seconds she was inside the posh car, heard faint sirens in the distance as the door closed behind her with a muted thud.

Trembling with the urge to throw herself at him and hug him, she turned to him. "Thank you."

He ignored that. "Are we waiting for them after all?"

"Oh, no." She fumbled for the ignition, discovered that the car was running, the motor so smooth it didn't produce sound or vibration. The car was such a dream to handle that even in her state, she drove to the nearest E.R. without incident.

As she parked, he turned to her. "Now drive home. I'll have the car and a driver at your disposal from now on."

He was almost out of the car before she flung herself after him. "I'm coming in with you."

His stare was even more spectacular in close quarters. "The deal was to drive me here, not escort me inside."

She clutched his arm tighter. "New deal, then."

"You have nothing to thank me for."

Now he answered her earlier thank you.

"I wasn't thanking you for saving my life, since I figured you'd have an allergic reaction to that. I was thanking you for letting me bargain with my safety for yours. Don't revert to being an aggravating superhero and insist on walking into the night alone."

After yet another long stare, he turned and exited the car.

Her heart constricted with disappointment and anxiety. If she persisted now, she'd be imposing on him.

Well, tough. That big, bad warrior would just have to use his endless stamina to put up with her concern.

The moment she was out of the car, her heart gave that boom that only he provoked. He was standing at the E.R. entrance, his pose worthy of the superhero she'd likened him to, one hand braced on his lean hips, the other still gripping her bloody scarf.

He was waiting for her.

She ran toward him, her heartbeat overtaking her feet.

Before she reached him, those cruelly sensuous lips twitched. Was that a smile? She wouldn't know. She'd never seen him smile.

Before she could make sure, he turned and strode inside.

He had her running to keep up with him, demonstrating that her concern was needless. *And* that he wouldn't make it easy for her to see her purpose through.

Once she knew he'd be okay, she'd show him exactly how much she'd put up with to be with him. That, if he let her, she would follow him to the ends of the earth.

Two

All through the admission process, Rashid felt Laylah's presence a breath away.

He couldn't take one without it mixing with the scent and heat of her body and her worry.

He found himself barely breathing so both wouldn't deluge him further. But rationing that involuntary act turned out to be easier than stopping another supposedly voluntary one. In spite of his intention to demonstrate that her presence was unnecessary as well as unimportant, his gaze kept going back to her like iron filings to a magnet. When no one, certainly never a woman, had ever commanded his unwilling response.

But Laylah Aal Shalaan wasn't anyone. There was no one else in the world that he remembered from the day of their birth.

He'd just turned eight when she was born, the first female offspring in the Aal Shalaan family in forty years. It had only been a week after he'd met her maternal *and* paternal cousins, Haidar and Jalal, and begun a friendship that had lasted for the next two decades.

She'd grown up under his gaze, always in his orbit, glowing

brighter every day with a radiance that had progressively dismayed him. He'd thought it so unfair, for her to be so matchlessly beautiful on the outside, when she could possess no beauty at all on the inside. Not when she was the daughter of a house of serpents.

Now that she'd matured, the injustice had been exacerbated.

His gaze returned to her again and again, documenting her every nuance. Hair and eyes the color of the richest chocolate and brushed with sunlight, skin of honeyed velvet and warm sunsets, a body of lush vitality and femininity and a face of a peculiar brand of splendor and harmony. But it was what those most unusual features radiated that perplexed him.

How could they transmit such…sweetness? Such…genuineness? The woman was descended from ruthless bitches and hardened criminals. There was no way any of that could be real.

Yet he was forced to believe one thing was real. Her concern for him. Its purity and intensity singed him.

But that could be explained away. By gratitude. To her lifeline in this harrowing experience. Once fright and shock drained away, so would her simulation of humanity and good nature.

Then he'd be free to resume thinking the worst of her. And treating her accordingly without the least remorse.

For now, he had to get out of her range. He needed to get his act together. To plan his next step.

"I'm coming with you."

At her blurted-out declaration, Rashid turned at the door of the treatment room. That eloquent eyebrow of his made her feel like an illogical species in the presence of a Vulcan.

He'd so far let her accompany him through the admission procedure. When the police had arrived, he'd fielded doubts about her being involved in the attack, lying with spectacular smoothness when they'd asked about her bruise.

According to him, it had been a basketball to the face during a one-on-two match with Mira—whom he'd always seen with her in the times she'd only sensed him—who'd back up anything she'd say. Just like the thugs would back up anything *he* said.

Not that those policemen would investigate any further. She had a feeling they realized the truth but seemed to appreciate his motivation for adjusting it wholeheartedly. They'd behaved as if they realized they were in the presence of a superior force who'd taken the pursuit of justice far beyond their level. The bare bones of his background had left them—and her—awed. They'd left the E.R. shaking his hand for what he'd done to those repeat offenders and slapping his back for how ruthlessly he'd done it.

It was the female E.R. doctor who answered her. "Only family members can accompany patients." She turned her awed eyes to Rashid. "Or if the patient specifically asks for your presence."

And you'd rather he didn't ask, Laylah almost retorted.

She tried cajoling, something she was abysmal at. "You've come this far. Might as well let me go all the way."

His eyes confirmed that she *had* failed to learn that survival mechanism as an endangered estrogen-based species in her family's testosterone jungle. Then he presented her with that unyielding back as he preceded the woman into the treatment room.

By the time thirty minutes had passed and more and more doctors had rushed into the room, she was certain they'd discovered his injury was catastrophic, and they'd been trying to contain the situation—and failing…

"I can't believe your luck, lady."

Laylah started, her nerves jangling. It was the E.R. nurse who'd first met them. She was exiting the treatment room.

Nurse Norma McGregor smiled widely at her. "Not that you were almost kidnapped, but that this god happened by and swooped in to save you."

She barely remembered Rashid's version in time. "Uh…that isn't what happened…"

"Oh, I know what he *said* happened, but I've seen the men he ripped apart. That had to be to punish what he'd consider a far more serious crime than attacking him. Attacking *you*. I also don't buy that story about your bruise. You two don't feel like you know each other enough for basketball. But don't worry. The boys in blue will swear on his version, so *we* can discuss the truth."

Laylah released the air trapped in her lungs. "You're uncanny at reading people."

Nurse McGregor tinkled a laugh. "Comes with the territory."

"I didn't want him to give the police a false statement…"

"But he insisted," Nurse McGregor put in. "And it makes him even more of a god. Shouldering this for you will save you no end of aggravation."

"Yeah. And he'd already saved me from far worse. If not for him, I would have been somewhere in the underbelly of Chicago by now, wondering if I'd survive. Instead, it was he who…who…" She had to stop as the tears finally began to flow.

Nurse McGregor frowned. "Hey, easy, girl. This is going to hit you hard when you process what happened and what *could* have happened. So don't fight it. Seek help."

Laylah wiped away her tears. "This isn't about my reaction. It's his wound…"

"Seeing that much blood disturbed you, huh?"

She shook her head. "I was a volunteer paramedic in my country. I've dealt with all kinds of injuries. But to see him hurt because he came to my defense…"

Comprehension dawned in the woman's blue eyes. "So it's because he's your knight in darkest armor that his superficial injury is making you so upset!"

"What superficial injury takes this long to take care of?" Laylah cried.

The woman waved. "Oh, his wound is long taken care of."

Laylah frowned. "So why are doctors rushing in there and not coming out?"

Nurse McGregor grinned. "That has nothing to do with *how* he is and everything to do with *who* he is."

"Huh?"

"You can't tell me you didn't notice the women fighting to take his case?"

She hadn't. With Rashid around, everything else in the world became inconsequential, almost invisible.

Nurse McGregor chuckled. "Well, they did, when normally they wouldn't be caught dead with such 'first-year-intern' injuries. Then Doctor Vergas threw her weight around as E.R. director and snapped him up." Laylah had noticed *that*. "Boy, did he give us a hard time, ordering us to get *him* sutures, saying he had more experience suturing wounds than all of us combined. But Doc Vergas convinced him to let her do it using the one thing she figured would get through to him."

"And that was?"

"You, of course."

"Huh?"

"She said if he didn't let her suture him, she'd have you come in to talk sense into him. He allowed her to sew him up without further resistance."

Oh.

He'd conceded only when threatened with the prospect of seeing *her?*

Was that good, bad or terrible?

Nurse McGregor sighed dramatically. "Even when he caved, he wouldn't take his sweater off, just raised it. But the inches we saw of him were…*whoa.*" A hand frantically fanned her face. "Maybe we wouldn't have survived seeing the whole package, after all."

TMI, Laylah almost blurted out. *TMDI. Too much* distressing *info.* She could do without more stimulation of her fantasies starring Rashid. Coupling concepts like "'all the way'" and "'the whole package'" with him wasn't good for her psychological health.

The woman went on. "Man, it's like he isn't human. First

that body, and then he didn't make a sound as we stitched him up when he'd refused local anesthesia or painkillers afterward. Then there's that *presence,* even when he didn't look at us or say a word."

Layla was intimate with Rashid's influence from lifelong experience. But... "All E.R. personnel *have* come out, including you. So who are those people who keep pouring into the room? What's going on?"

"That's what I meant when I said it's all about who he is. After we were done, he said he'd make a donation to the department. Then he mentioned a number. That's when we E.R personnel stampeded out, to spread the word and investigate him on the internet And we found out exactly *who* we have in there."

That must have been a shock. Rashid was worth a few dozen billions. Men of his caliber had entire hospitals at their beck and call and health insurance that would airlift them anywhere in the world if they sprained their ankle. It was actually odd that he'd consented to go to a regular E.R., even for a "glorified paper cut."

Nurse McGregor flicked her head toward the room. "So those illustrious figures you saw storming in there? They're department heads, each trying to sell him on a project that needs funding."

He was in there talking *business?* Leaving her out here going out of her mind?

With a smile that must be as brittle as her nerves, she said, "Thanks for the recap and everything else, Nurse McGregor."

Then she marched into that till-now off-limits room.

Sure enough, Rashid *was* swarmed.

Not that he appeared concerned. Even surrounded by people like a rock star by groupies, he towered a head over everyone, that vast energy he emitted engulfing the scene. He was wearing only his bloody slate-gray sweater. His coat was hooked carelessly from a finger over his back.

She'd thought that coat had made him more imposing. But stripped of its obscuring folds, the symmetry and strength that infused his every line, the power and perfection that filled and strained against the cashmere, ruined as it was, were…

What had the nurse said? Yeah. *Whoa.*

No wonder *god* had been the only word the woman had found to describe him. He did look the part, presiding over his worshippers with all the contained might and forbearance of one.

He saw her the second she entered. In fact, his gaze had been pinned on the door.

Had he been expecting her to disobey hospital rules? But that wasn't what had kept her out. It had been his unspoken, and this time non-negotiable, demand. So had he been expecting her to disregard his wishes? And had he been watching the door so intently because he'd been worried she would? Or only as his means of escape from those who would devour him whole?

There was no way to read the answer on that heart-wrenchingly gorgeous face he wore like a mask. But she let him read her own thoughts in the gaze that clashed with his.

His response was to raise that eyebrow in a calm, *Still here?*

She folded her arms over her chest, letting him know he could spend the night holed up in here, wheeling and dealing, and she'd stand right here and wait for him to be done.

A glint in his fathomless eyes acknowledged he was aware of her intention.

Then he turned his gaze to the man standing closest to him. "Mr. Hendrix, please send your proposal to my corporation's email with E.R. in the subject line. I'll get back to you within two weeks." Voices rose, trying to get the same offer. He cut them all short. "Give Mr. Hendrix your proposals. I'll do what I can."

Without one further look at anyone, he walked away. She could see they wanted to cling to him, but there was no way anyone could stand in Rashid's way once he'd made up his mind. They parted for him like the Red Sea for Moses.

He didn't slow down as he reached her, only inclined his

head at her as he exited the room, his earlier silent inquiry now a statement. "You didn't leave."

She hurried after him, stumbling on legs that felt mismatched as his scent, even over the overpowering hospital smells, filled her lungs. "You thought I would?"

He spared her a sideways glance from his prodigious height. "You should have."

"Yeah, right." Her gaze flitted to the pristine white bandage peeking below what now looked like viscous ink on his sweater. She felt nauseated that his flesh had been torn, again, this time for her.

"Are you all right?" she asked. Her breathlessness had nothing to do with almost running to match his endless strides.

He gave her a look that pointed out that she was the one having trouble keeping up. "I don't look it?"

You look more than all right. You look divine.

She barely bit back the words. "Looks can be deceiving. Especially yours."

Both eyebrows rose this time. "I wish I'd known I had chameleonlike powers before. That would have come in handy during my black ops days."

So after being a war hero he'd veered into ultimate warrior territory. A natural progression, really. Only the most formidable soldiers made it and survived in that utmost-skill, maximum-peril world.

Had that been what had shaped him into this force of darkness? He'd always been complex, but his current depths must have been forged in experiences she couldn't even imagine. The brutal demands and dangers of a black ops life fit the bill.

She cleared her tightening throat. "I meant your skin. It's so…" *Polished and bronzed and tough, so touchable…so lickable…* She clamped down on the overheating thoughts. "Tanned. Anyone less…opaque would be pale as a ghost from blood loss by now."

His eyes moved dismissively away. "It's clear you've never seen what blood loss looks like."

She quickened her steps to capture his fixed-ahead gaze. "I do now. I was a volunteer paramedic through college in Zohayd."

Had she managed to stun him again? That she could decipher a flicker in his eyes meant that she had. And then some.

Did it surprise him that much that she'd volunteered, and in such an occupation? Was he surprised to discover she wasn't what her mother had tried so hard to make her—a pampered pawn?

"Then you must know all this blood only looks dramatic. I've got liters still circulating about, doing its job, and the loss is merely an incentive for my body to produce a replacement, something I've always found revitalizing."

Her jaw dropped. "You find blood loss *revitalizing?*"

"It does jog my body out of a rut. Before you wonder, I don't have proclivities for inflicting it on myself for kicks, but when it does happen, I look at the bright side."

She and Nurse McGregor had been right. There *was* something more than human about him.

"You're still not convinced, even when your paramedical experience is telling you I'm right."

He was. But… "I—I just can't stop thinking how much worse it could have been…"

"But it wasn't. You can stop guilt-tripping."

He was wrong about *that*. It wasn't guilt. It was this…fear for him, even when she knew that danger had been averted.

He sighed. "What will convince you that I won't keel over? I assure you I don't intend to for roughly the next fifty years."

The out-of-nowhere flashes of his dry-as-tinder sense of humor amazed her.

Her lips quivered. "I'll hold you to that."

Another sideways glance, longer this time, and even more unsettling. But he said nothing more as he navigated out of the hospital and into the freezing night.

She fought the urge to take his hand as they crossed the road. Driving him here and escorting him inside were two things he'd grudgingly consented to. Literally holding his hand was another level of infringement altogether. And she'd rather not be exposed to more eyebrow action.

But she was, in response to her rushing to take the wheel.

He reinforced that eyebrow's censure by remaining outside, his bulk blocking the passenger-side window.

A button wound it down. "Get in already."

He only stood there, uncaring of the icy wind as his coat flowed around him like a magician's cape. "You'd rather drive yourself home instead of giving me directions?"

She thought of saying yes, just so he'd get in from the cold. But even if she didn't suffer from advanced candor, she wouldn't bargain with him with anything less than the full truth.

She looked up at him with her unequivocal intention. "I'm driving *you* home."

Widening his stance, he shoved his hands in his pants' pockets, evidently having no problem with haggling over this all night. "Our deal wasn't open-ended. It ended when you heard with your own ears that my injury was trivial."

"So the injury wasn't as bad as you're used to, and the blood loss turned out to be a kick. But the stitches must be hurting like hell, especially since you went all Rambo and refused anesthesia *and* painkillers. Even if you have an inhuman pain threshold and feel nothing, bottom line is, I'm still driving. *And* I won't just drop you home and leave. I'm coming in with you."

That silenced him. For at least thirty seconds.

Then he leaned down, looked straight into her eyes, the night of his own eyes deep enough to engulf her whole.

Slowly, distinctly, he said, "I've been in three wars, princess. I forget how many other lesser scale, if sometimes even more vicious, armed conflicts. Not to mention all those missions I undertook with one-way tickets because coming back at all, let alone in one piece, was a one in a hundred shot at best. I've seen and done and had done to me some of the absolute worst things imaginable. Two-dozen stitches actually feels nostalgic now that I've left the battlefield behind for the boardroom. I assure you, I can tuck myself into bed."

That image filled her with heat. How many women had fought for that privilege, had had that pleasure…?

She bit her lip at the disconcerting projections. "I'm sure you can also lug the whole world on your back, Sheikh Atlas. But that doesn't mean that you have to, or that you have to do it alone. No matter what, you're not alone tonight. You got those stitches in my defense, so that makes them mine, too, and I have an equal right in deciding how to view them. You think they're negligible or nostalgic, I think they're premium grounds for fussing. You evidently find being fussed over an alien concept, but you'll have to suck it up, since fuss over you I will. So you might as well give in, get in and let me take you home."

Judging by the infinitesimal widening of his eyes, she'd definitely flabbergasted him. She'd bet no one had ever dared talk to him like that.

When he finally spoke, his voice was an octave deeper, if that was possible, "I really don't need—"

"I know you need nothing from anyone." Now that she had him miraculously off-balance, she had to strike the red-hot iron of his indecision and get the obdurate man in from the cold. "It's a given you can take care of yourself at the absolute worst of times, having done so all your life. But you won't tonight. Tonight, I take care of you."

Three

She'd pushed her luck too far.

From the way Rashid was looking at her, as if she were an alien life form, she feared she'd done worse. Instead of persuading him to get into the car, she might have convinced him to walk home on foot.

What the hell. Might as well go all the way.

She leaned farther so she could look up at him. "If you're thinking of calling a cab, I'll follow it. If you decide to walk, I'll cruise along beside you. Or I'll get out and walk with you and you'll have my hypothermia on your hands and your conscience."

He clearly couldn't believe his ears.

She grinned up at him. *Stick around and, according to my family, you'll hear plenty of pretty unbelievable stuff.*

Before she could utter another word he was in the car, and she sat back quickly into her seat, stunned by how fast he had moved.

She blinked at him. How could someone of his height and

bulk flow so effortlessly? It was as if he had a stealth mode and tricked her senses into not registering his movement.

Had they taught him that in black ops training? Or were those powers of undetectability why he'd been sought for the position in the first place?

After closing the window, he presented her with his profile. Not even his horrific scar detracted from its hewn perfection.

Ya Ullah, but he was utter beauty.

Her one complaint was that he'd almost shaved off his hair. She'd once made a profound study of how its lush silkiness framed his masterpiece of a face, how its virile hairline outlined his lion's forehead, how it captured light only to emit it in glimmers of raven gloss. She'd been grateful when he'd kept growing it so there'd been more of it for her to delight in. When she'd been twelve or thirteen, he'd worn it in a ponytail midway down his back. She'd lived for the times when he'd unbound it.

Even when he'd joined the army, he hadn't gotten a military cut. But now he had barely half an inch to adorn his warrior's head. That was an injustice of massive proportions.

Burning to ask why he kept it so ruthlessly cropped, she waited for him to say something. Like where to drive.

His continued silence told her she should figure out what to do with the rest of her one-sided plan. *He'd* contribute nothing more.

She started the ignition, cranked up the heater, turned back to him. "I'll need directions."

Without a word, he set the GPS then resumed his position.

So. The silent treatment. Two could play at this game.

Twenty minutes later, cruising the powerful car down almost-empty streets on the outskirts of the city, she'd long realized that *that* was easier bragged about than achieved.

She'd spent a lifetime yearning to talk to him and failing. Now she wanted to make up for all of those frustrating times. She wanted to deluge him with a thousand questions, yammer on about all the things she'd longed to say to him all her life.

But his silence was like a barrier. It made her awareness of him highly distressing. She felt as if his every breath expanded in her own chest, as if every impulse powering his magnificent body quivered through her nerves.

Then she felt him slide a discreet glance her way.

She tore her gaze from the road to his face. For a fraction of a second she saw something...unguarded.

It was gone before she could latch on to it, but she felt he was wrestling with something. Irritation? Humor? What?

"You understand that was blackmail."

All her hairs, perpetually at half-mast around him, stood on end as the velvet night of his voice poured into her ear.

Her lips wobbled. "I choose to call it persistence. In response to your pointless resistance."

"My resistance wasn't pointless. Just useless."

Her grin widened as she returned her eyes to the road. "That it was. But pray tell, what *was* its point?"

"That you shouldn't be with me. That it's inappropriate."

"Oh, no. You're not pulling our region's traditions on me, of what's 'appropriate' behavior for women, especially the variety stigmatized by spinsterhood."

"You're not a spinster."

Her laugh dripped in sarcasm. "Tell that to my family, especially my dear mother. I've been a spinster in her eyes for over ten years."

"Ten years ago you were a child of seventeen."

He knew her age!

She tried not to grin like a fool at the discovery. "And I was already past my prime then. You know girls in our region are expected to interest men in acquiring them earlier than that."

Instead of debating her, he only said, "Any reason why you don't find this situation inappropriate?"

Was he for real? "Because we're not in Azmahar or Zohayd?"

"Our behavior shouldn't change based on geography. Wherever we are, we remain who we are. You—more than anyone from our region—should always observe said 'traditions.' As you realized tonight, they're not only set to limit your freedom, but to protect you."

"You're *not* saddling me with the responsibility for tonight's attack. Tonight was a fluke…"

"You can't afford flukes. Or to think that guards would 'cramp your style.'"

"Is that why you think I don't have guards? Seems you haven't kept abreast with the latest developments."

"Why don't you update me?"

"Sure. Where did you last leave off the soap opera that is my family life? You know the basics, how the whole mess started. Two brothers marrying two sisters to unite two kingdoms, and instead of being satisfied with their enviable lots of wealth, status and healthy children, becoming each others' worst enemies."

His gaze plunged into his own realizations. "You discovered how things stood between your parents, and your uncle and aunt."

"Only from the time I knew who they were."

That she'd always known seemed to interest him. At least she thought that was what that last heavy-lidded glance signified.

She sighed. "Then it all came to an inevitably explosive end when my mother and aunt plotted against their husbands and got caught, divorced and exiled. That's where the part about my guards comes in. All my life, until her exile, my mother was obsessed with one thing. That she, the lofty Princess Somayah of Azmahar, not end up as a second-rate princess, known only for being sister to Queen Sondoss of Zohayd and married to King Atef's brother. She had me hounded by a platoon to safeguard the asset she hoped would bring her an alliance that would elevate her to her sister's higher royal status, and rid her of dependence on my father's family. My father, who's always been mired in gold-digging mistresses, only sent guards after me to evict hers in his petty feud with her. Once their toxic relationship was thankfully over, they dismissed me from their minds, the one thing they'd rather forget bonded them forever. So, I've been guard-free since I left Zohayd."

His jaw hardened. "Why didn't you ask your uncle Atef or your cousins for replacements? Why don't you hire some yourself?"

"I never ask anyone for anything, let alone round-the-clock protection. And while my software development business is taking off, my liquid assets are tied up in its operating capital. Most important, I really felt I didn't need protection. I came here to start a new life as just another single woman living in the city. I paid attention to my safety. This was the first time I ran into any trouble."

"It only takes once."

She exhaled. "True. But it didn't happen because I was negligent. Someone was determined to hurt me. They would have found a way no matter what I did. And I'm grateful you happened along."

A long moment of silence followed her statement.

At length, he exhaled. "As a princess of Zohayd, you must never be without protection. And you should never be with a strange man, let alone offer to drive him home."

Oh, man. He *was* going all protective and disapproving on her. As if she needed to find him any yummier.

"You *are* strange—" in a uniquely and incredibly exciting way, her grin told him "—but not a stranger."

That majestic head inclined in delicious curtness. "Not a *total* stranger, granted, but still one."

"Oh, come on, Rashid. Next you're going to say I need a *mehrem*." In other words, an adult male of her kin whom she couldn't marry to chaperone her in the presence of males she could. "How about you stop behaving as if we don't know each other?"

"We don't."

A huff of incredulity burst out at his emphatic declaration. "Yeah, right. I've known you all my life."

"You've seen me from afar for a portion of it."

"Yeah, a portion comprising its first seventeen years. And the 'from afar' bit was your doing. It sure wasn't for lack of trying to come closer on my part."

There. Her crass candor was getting into gear. But boy, had she tried to come closer.

She'd tried to be everywhere he was while he'd been in Zohayd, had found every reason to be in Azmahar when he'd been there, striving for a chance to talk to him. Yet no matter her ingenuity, she could count on one hand the quasi-exchanges they'd ever had. The one thing ameliorating her disappointment had been that Rashid was like that with *everyone*. Not that he'd been *that* reserved with others. And not that she'd ever given up.

After he'd joined the army and his appearances had become more sporadic, she'd obsessively done everything she could to be around for the rare visits. But war between Azmahar and Damhoor had erupted mere months after he'd enlisted. Then he'd been reported missing and thought dead....

Ya Ullah, she'd never known such desperation. Or such relief when he'd turned up weeks later, alive and leading his squad back to civilization. She'd almost died of frustration when she hadn't been able to go with Haidar and Jalal to greet him at his return. But she'd gone to the ceremony where he'd received Azmahar's highest medal of valor. She'd still had to ambush him to congratulate him, tell him how thankful she'd been for his safety. But he'd been more aloof than ever before.

He'd drifted farther away from then on until he'd seemed to disappear off the face of the earth. He'd resurfaced almost three years ago, just as the upheaval in Zohayd had erupted, as her closest cousins', Haidar's and Jalal's, enemy, and subsequently the enemy of her whole family.

No one knew what had happened between the former best friends to tear them apart so viciously. She didn't even know if it was the same thing that had alienated Haidar and Jalal themselves. All she'd known was that she had to be resigned that *she* would never see him again. That she'd never had any chance with him, anyway.

Now fate had brought him exploding back into her life, only for her to find he'd become this exhilarating delight of a man who was still making her struggle for every inch closer…

The GPS announced that they'd arrived at their destination.

Bringing the car to a stop, she squinted up through the windshield.

He lived in a…warehouse?

His next words confirmed it. "Now that you've driven me home, I'll have someone tail you to yours."

She took the key out and handed it to him. When he wouldn't take it, she placed it on his lap and took off her seat belt. "Which part of 'I'm taking care of you tonight' didn't you get?"

His gaze bathed her in such calm contemplation it had blood fizzing in her ears. "This comes from being one of the two prized female Aal Shalaans, right?"

"Uh…what does?"

"The expectation that men will do your bidding. You're used to saying 'jump' only for your male kin to ask 'how high?'"

One thing for sure, *she'd* jump if only he said to. She'd stay in the air until he said down, too.

No need to tell him that just yet. For now, she'd let him believe she was an old hand at getting her way. If he believed she was more effective than she really was, it made it more likely she'd sway him, too. Good press was everything, after all.

She smiled. "Invite me in, Rashid."

"That's an ill-advised demand, princess."

"Will you stop with this 'princess' business? You'd better, if you don't want me to 'sheikh' you."

"'Sheikh' away. Boundaries are essential."

She rolled her eyes. "Whatever. Can we take our boundaries inside? I'm dying for a cup of tea. I promise to make you one."

"I don't drink tea."

He didn't, huh? She might just discover he didn't eat food, either, his sustenance being evil souls. And he'd already gorged on four for dinner.

"You must have other beverages in your place."

"Tap water."

Her lips twisted. "You won't put me off, you know."

"I'm stating facts."

"Next you'll say you have nothing to eat but dried dates."

His shrug should have been immortalized on video as the template for nonchalance. "It's not far from the truth."

Water and dates, huh? The sustenance of desert nomads. It actually fit that he, having lived years in survival mode through hardships and deprivation the likes of which she couldn't imagine, would be programmed to exist on the bare necessities. Even now that he was a billionaire, he hadn't gone soft or become dependent upon modern comforts and conveniences. He might drive a car only his kind of money could buy, but he reverted to his adversity-thriving true self in a heartbeat.

We remain who we are, no matter where we are.

And who he was, was the best thing she'd ever known.

She grinned into his brooding eyes. "Water and dates work for me."

"Fine. You can come in." Not much of an invitation, but she'd take it. She was sizzling with eagerness to. At least, she was before he doused it. "Until your escort arrives."

Before she could object, he was out of the car in yet another impossibly effortless move.

Her exit wasn't as graceful, nor was her progress to catch up with him at the door of what looked like a deserted warehouse below an equally empty, old, industrial-looking brick building.

As he pointed a remote at the huge steel door, she nodded at the deserted area. "See this? There's no one around like there always is in our region. No malicious eyes to monitor my visit or wagging tongues to weave it into a scandal. Why are you worried?"

"Why aren't you?"

"Because I can't worry about anything with you around. Because I feel safer with you than I ever did in my life. Why else?"

Another episode of inertness descended on him. She was quickly learning that indicated astonishment. Even shock.

His next words reinforced that belief, his eyes narrowing a fraction. "You believe I pose no danger of any sort?"

"Definitely not to me." The words were out before she realized he might mean a different kind of danger...the sexual kind.

If only. With this avenging archangel, she was safer in that arena than she was in her currently all-female environment. A depressing thought if any ever was.

He pressed the remote and the door opened with the whirr of a perfectly oiled machine, belying its weather-beaten appearance.

Before he turned away, he belatedly commented on her wholehearted assertion. "Interesting."

You can say that again, she thought, watching the receding streetlights paint shadows across his back as he forged deeper into the darkness, a sorcerer becoming one with his lair.

He left the lights off. On purpose, she was sure, to rattle her. Punishing her for behaving so "inappropriately"?

Too bad for him it wouldn't work. Not only did she have no fear of darkness, it was true she'd fear nothing with him by her side. Maybe they did lack some knowledge of one another that closer interaction would have fostered, but she did know the essential him. His essence had touched hers so profoundly that he starred in her very first memory.

Deciding to call him out on his efforts to intimidate her, she said, "Let there be light, Rashid. Only so neither of us breaks a toe against a cabinet or something."

At her mockery, there *was* light. Not a sudden burst, but a dawning of golden, sourceless illumination so gradual her vision didn't have to adjust to take in her surroundings. A vast, 30-foot-ceilinged warehouse-to-loft conversion. There was one word for it: Spartan. She now truly knew what the word meant. It was this: a warrior's dwelling. Sparse, utilitarian, austere. It was also more. A piece of ancient Azmahar, before oil and technology had transformed its distinctive heritage into yet another twenty-first-century Westernized hybrid. Every line and surface, and what little furniture there was, was steeped in Azmahar's history, bearing the stamp of its authenticity in a muted palette of desert-inspired tones.

"Of course." She realized she'd said that out loud when he turned to her. "Now that I've seen this place, I realize nothing else—and nothing less—could have suited you. Or…contained you."

"Contained me?" His gaze swept the place before he leveled that bone-melting stare back on her. "Quite the bottle, isn't it?"

A laugh burst out of her. "You do fit the genie profile. Especially with the way you materialized out of thin air tonight."

Shrugging out of his coat, he moved deeper into the huge space. "I'm sure that satisfies your sense of dramatic license far more than the mundane explanation."

Removing her coat as well and following him farther into the room, she faced him as he stopped before a fireplace and held out her arms for the logs he'd picked up. "I'll do that. You sit down."

"So it's not 'jump' this time, but 'sit,' eh? What next? Roll over? Beg?"

A chuckle bubbled out as she tried to imagine him doing any of that. But the funny actions only turned to licentious images in her head. Oh, the *images*.

Trapping a moan, she grinned. "Maybe. And maybe I'll ask you to jump to that mezzanine. I bet you can jump tall buildings in a single bound. But even superheroes need to put their feet up once in a while. As you're going to do tonight."

Without a shadow of a smile in return, he handed her the logs and left her to start a fire. He sank down on top of a woolen *kelim* woven in Azmahar's national colors and motifs. Leaning on one of two huge complementing cushions, he proceeded to watch her like a black panther would contemplate a contrary gazelle.

His gaze made her more distressed with each breath; its touch unleashing impulses she'd believed would be forever banked with him forever out of her life.

As he would be after tonight.

But tonight was still here. As was she. And she would make the most out of this windfall.

With the fire going, she turned to him. "You're hungry."

"I am?"

"Judging by your size and muscle mass, you must require quite a lot of sustenance frequently. It's been almost four hours since you came to my rescue. So yes, you're hungry now."

It could have been the play of firelight. But she could swear an obsidian flame started flickering in the depths of his eyes.

He inclined his head, casting his face in deeper shadow, depriving her of closer investigation. "So you don't just order your males around, you tell them how they feel, too."

"'My males?'" A laugh overcame her. "*Ya Ullah,* what a concept." His intensity ratcheted up until she had to look away, had to walk to the open-plan kitchen at the far end of the gigantic space. "So…food. Please tell me I'll find something more than water and dates in there."

"I can still call someone to follow you home now rather than later."

"No, thanks." Arriving at the kitchen, she looked around. "You weren't exaggerating, were you? No fridge? So how do you eat? Out? Or do you exist on takeaway? Or have a cook come in regularly?"

"No cook. I get fresh ingredients delivered daily, use them up, rinse and repeat."

That actually sounded like a very healthy way to live. He *was* the picture of vigor and virility, so he was doing it right. Very.

She leaned across the island, luxuriated in watching him coming closer. "So where's today's consignment?"

He stopped before her. "I intended to have dinner out."

"Until me."

"Until you."

The way he said those words… Was there tenderness in his tone, or was it her imagination again?

She cleared her tight throat. "So how am I supposed to feed you? You don't even have dates, do you?"

"I have all kinds of dried fruits." He pointed toward the cup-
boards behind her.

"I can use those. For dessert. For the main course, I bet you
can get anything delivered at any time."

He brooded at her for what felt like an hour.

Her gaze began to waver. He was going to outstare her and...

He suddenly looked heavenward, as if asking the fates just
what they'd thrown in his path tonight. Then he inhaled sharply,
exhaled as forcefully.

Wow. She'd done it. She'd dragged a full-blown reaction out
of him. A *human* one, to boot.

Her internal celebration hiccupped as he recaptured her in
the crosshairs of his focus. "Fine. I'll have whatever ingredients you require delivered. What do you want to feed me?"

She barely managed not to jump and pump a fist into the air.

Another minibattle won!

Her smile was so wide she doubted her lips would revert to
their former size. "What do *you* want to eat?"

In response, he produced his cell phone, called someone
named Ahmad then handed her the phone.

As he walked away he said over his shoulder, "Surprise me.
You're superlative at it, after all."

Four

Surprise had long given way to ever-expanding disbelief as Rashid watched Laylah prowling all over his place, "taking care of him." She was now in his kitchen again, preparing him dessert.

This was not going according to plan.

Why was he *letting* her do this to him? He should be the one setting the pace, calling the shots.

Yet, since she'd pounced on him with her scarf and concern in that alley, he'd been letting her steer him. And this alien experience of being taken care of only got more…incapacitating.

No one had ever done anything like this for him, to him. He'd never let anyone near enough to even try. Not even Haidar and Jalal. He'd once rejected all their efforts to impose their brand of caring on him. He'd since lived happily alone.

Zain. So "happily" didn't apply. He had no idea what happiness was. He'd heard people describe it. He'd observed them living it. It was what Haidar and Jalal appeared to be eyeballs-deep in now, with their brides. He'd never experienced anything remotely resembling their conditions and he'd been fiercely thankful for that. They'd been...compromised. Their power was no longer their own; their priorities forever messed up. He'd been unwavering in his belief that he wasn't equipped to succumb to anything like that so-called happiness, that there was nothing to jog his ironclad order and intentions. Happiness, and everything else that people wanted, was for other men. Men with no mission.

Then tonight had happened. *She* had happened.

Laylah Aal Shalaan. This...*shock.*

Instead of the self-centered and self-serving spoiled witch he'd expected her to be, a budding edition of her black-hearted mother and aunt, there was this...being who seemed to exude a pristine nature and an overwhelming generosity of spirit. He'd spent the past hours looking for chinks in her act. He'd found none.

So he was floundering. Not only because she was not following the script he'd had in mind but because *he* wasn't.

He kept doing the opposite of what he'd intended to do. He kept doing everything in his power to sabotage his own plans.

Instead of grabbing this opportunity that had hurled itself at him, he'd found himself shaking it off as if it burned him. He'd done everything to push her away, when he'd been following her for weeks, planning how to get close. She'd had to push him and pull at him until he'd let her come here. When he should have suggested it, or at least not fought against it with all he had.

But he *had* fought her every step of the way, his resistance becoming fiercer the more she'd clung. He'd tried all he could to talk her out of giving him what he'd planned to manipulate her into.

So no, nothing was going as planned. Everything was going *far* better than anything he'd dared hope for.

And that more than disturbed him.

He'd never been in a situation like this. He always had a plan, then followed it to the last meticulous detail. Whenever he seemed to be improvising brilliantly, he was only following one of the contingencies he'd made allowances for.

The only time he hadn't done that to the letter, he'd almost paid with his life. He *had* paid with his mutilation.

Even then, he hadn't veered off his planned course that far. He'd never let anything or anyone sabotage his plans that much.

But she was doing so by setting his plans on hyperdrive. What he'd hope to achieve in weeks had been condensed into hours. He hadn't needed a strategy to get her where he wanted her. He was the one who needed to come to terms with how fast his plan was working when he hadn't even meant to initiate it. He was the one who was wondering what had hit him. The one who had to struggle to catch his breath.

Her enthusiasm might turn out to be as deleterious to his plans as her flat-out rejection could have been. Being so uncharted and unpredictable, it could prove even more catastrophic.

His heart thudded as she flashed him a smile before resuming her work, humming some merry tune.

Maybe he was overthinking it. Maybe he should not question his good luck.

But how could he not? Nothing like this had ever happened to him. He'd never been exposed to anyone like her. Was it any wonder he had no skill set in place to handle it or her?

And *that* was why he was succumbing to her coddling. He kept searching through his head for a method to regain control of the situation. But he found no precedent with which to deal with her.

The paradox was that she was overriding him with the sheer force of her…openness, her guilelessness. Her eagerness. Three qualities he had no experience with.

He should be using her willingness to do anything for him, her unwillingness to leave him, to his advantage.

Yet said advantage was the last thing on his mind. Thinking at all wasn't among his capabilities right now. His faculties were all engaged in surrendering to whatever she wished to do, for him, to him. In dreading the time when she had to leave.

These unknown reactions could be due to blood loss after all. Or the brush with resurrected insanity.

He watched her move toward him, her undulations the essence of femininity, yet not in the least studied, as spontaneous as everything else about her. Her face was open for him to read, the smile that spread those full, flushed lips transmitting something he'd never thought to see. Pure pleasure at being with him. And it wasn't gratitude. It was far more. He couldn't think how this could be.

But why think? Or analyze why she wanted to be here, why *he* wanted her here? Why everything was going so perfectly? It *was* an alien concept, but maybe he should just go along with it.

Maybe this time, having his original plan destroyed wouldn't end in disaster.

"I've discovered one thing you're *not* superlative at!"

At her triumphant declaration, Rashid raised his eyes in utmost deliberateness from the bowl he'd just wiped clean.

Anyone would have quaked under the impact of his gaze.

Laylah did quake. With an excitement that was getting harder to contain. Being with him was like being hooked to a source of inexhaustible energy. Like being infused with a narcotic, an upper. She did feel high. On him. On life, now that he was near.

Her delight had soared as she'd engaged him in repartee until the delivery of her requested items, then as she'd prepared them. When he'd sauntered into the kitchen and started working alongside her, she'd run to fetch a cushion, placed it where she'd have the best view of him and patted it. He'd stood there staring at that cushion, the picture of disbelief.

When he'd finally grumbled that this was worse than black ops conditioning, she'd spluttered in laughter. Hilarity had become fierce sweetness as that indomitable force had sat down where she'd indicated, letting her have this pleasure.

And pleasure it had been, the likes of which she'd never experienced. She'd never enjoyed cooking as she had for him, never enjoyed eating as she had with him. And then there had been the delight of watching him devour everything she'd prepared, and listening to his rumbles of enjoyment as he'd demolished the honey-glazed salmon, sautéed vegetables and avocado-based salad.

He'd just finished the *khoshaaf* she'd made soaking dried fruits in honeyed water and topping them with toasted almonds and spices. He'd scooped the last drops of syrup as if he'd coax the bowl to give up more, showing her how much he wished there was. He'd been vocally appreciative of her effort and not a little stunned at her skill. He'd admitted he'd thought he'd have to suffer ingesting whatever she'd imagined passed for cooking and be done with it. As it was, he could have eaten ten times as much. Not that he'd accepted second helpings. He'd insisted he never ate that much at a time, nor that elaborately.

Every word, no matter how it betrayed his preconceptions of her, had been a caress to her heart.

Now he was waiting for her to qualify her statement that there was something he wasn't perfect at.

"Math," she elaborated. "You counted the 'prized female Aal Shalaans' wrong. I've been one of *three* for a while now."

Those divinely sculpted lips curled on that pout/twist combo that made her inside quiver. Her fingers itched to explore their dips and swells, her lips their...

He interrupted the cascade of imagery. "*Aih,* since discovering that Aliyah, now queen of Judar, is one. I hear she, too, had perfected the art of twisting untwistable men around her little finger."

That, too, made her smile widen. "If you mean King Kamal, the twisting is mutual, I assure you."

His gaze was dismissal itself. "Whatever you say."

She took the bowl from his relaxed hands. "Why count on my word? One look at them would tell you they're both equally smitten."

Leaning back against the wall at the dining area—another floor arrangement with only a *tubbleyah,* a one-foot-high, unfinished-wood, round table, another *keleem* and a couple more megacushions—he crossed now-bare feet at the ankles. "Women of Aliyah's caliber can wreak untold havoc. But she must have her hard life to thank for her ability to rein in her lethal potential. Her family's indulgence was so misguided that it almost destroyed her body and mind. After struggling to overcome the damage they did, she must have learned control, not to mention compassion for others. That makes Kamal one lucky wretch."

His eyes challenged her to find a credible answer to his evaluation.

Instead, she held her hand down to him.

His gaze moved to it but he did not take it.

Not willing to accept a hand up from her? Guess she'd pushed her luck again, this time right into his comfort zone.

Hand prickling with the letdown, she withdrew it—only for it to be snagged in a vise of sheer power: his warm, beautiful, tough hand.

A thousand sensations coursed through her. Tears prickled behind her eyes at the exquisiteness of each.

Earlier, he'd *had* to touch her. This was his first voluntary touch, an answer to her request to let her closer. An acceptance she'd only dreamed of having. Every impulse strained to pull that hand that had been bruised in her defense to her lips, to worship every knuckle and callus.

A gasp escaped from her throat, as without tugging on her, just by tightening his grip, he was on his feet, towering over her. He was so close—his heat and scent flooded her, his aura cloaked her. For a haywire series of heartbeats she thought he'd…

He only stood there, looking down at their joined hands.

Then he raised them along with that delightful eyebrow. "Where do you want me now?"

Anywhere. Everywhere. As long as you're in my life.

Good thing she wasn't *that* candid. Not yet. No need to scare the poor man this early on.

Showing him where she wanted him for now, she led him back to the fireplace. Once he was seated again, she ran to the kitchen and brought him a mug of hot hibiscus tea, which he accepted with a direct gaze that she now knew meant he found no point in resisting anymore and would let her run her coddling routine with no more objections. If he'd had hair for her to ruffle, she would have ventured to do so.

She settled for a teasing smile as she sat beside him. "I've heard of being damned by faint praise, but you damn by the fervent variety. You included me when you mentioned women of a certain 'caliber,' right? And analyzing why Aliyah didn't become a weapon of mass destruction was your roundabout way of telling me that because *I* was spoiled rotten, I remain deadly?"

He raised his mug to her in salutation of her accuracy. "If the roundabout way offends you, my apologies."

Her head pitched back on a laugh. His wit, what he let her see of it, tickled her. What would it be like fully unleashed?

"Apologies will only be accepted if you stop burning calories skirting issues. It's all I'll ever ask of you, to be truthful with me. Always. I will never be anything but that with you."

It was a long moment before he raised his eyes from the steaming depths of his drink. "If you think you can handle it."

"Oh, you have no idea what I can handle." She gave him a quirked eyebrow. "I hope you can take it as well as dish it out?"

"What do you think?" Those black lasers he had for eyes told her exactly what to think. "But I attempted a watered-down approach for my own sake. I hear your species subsists on a steady diet of fawning and flattery, and I wasn't up to saving you again if an injection of the truth sent you into anaphylactic shock."

At her hoot of delight, he continued watching her over the rim of his mug, taking more tranquil sips.

Wiping away tears, she rose to her knees, facing him. "Sir, you misjudge my species. Understandable, since it's undocu-

mented with me as its only member. The fluke female Aal
Shalaan. Of which you know nothing, according to you. I guess
all knowledge *is* on my side. I bet you never noticed I existed
before tonight."

A bolt of black lightning arced from his eyes.

Did that mean he *had* noticed her? When? How hadn't *she*
noticed, when she'd been analyzing his every nuance, scaveng-
ing for any sign of interest or attention?

She let out a choppy exhalation. "So you noticed me? And
still think I was indulged? What on earth did you observe in
my family's treatment of me that could have been mistaken for
indulgence? You thought my mother keeping me practically on
a leash was that? Or my father making any excuse he could
think of to escape giving me five minutes of his time? Or both
using me as a pawn in their maneuvers with everyone else or
a weapon in their own ongoing war?"

He frowned. She hadn't seen him do that when he'd been
about to kill her attackers; then, she had only seen that scarily
empty expression.

But now she felt something emanating from him, far dead-
lier than the rage he'd exuded earlier tonight.

Wow. Was this in response to her account of how her parents had treated her? She hadn't meant to sound bitter, but in
reality, she'd "watered things down." Not that she'd thought to
appeal to his sympathy. Whatever she'd suffered at her parents' self-serving hands had been nothing compared to what
he'd suffered.

Needing to lighten the mood, she infused her voice with
extra lightness. "Or maybe you believed I was indulged because my legions of cousins didn't rough me up like they did
each other? That had nothing to do with my being female, just
being the youngest."

As if consenting to play along, his lips twisted. "I didn't
see those who succeeded you to that position being spared,
since these were disappointingly male. You can't deny the Aal
Shalaans' situation goes against everything our region believes

in. Instead of valuing males above females for offspring, having nothing but sons made the Aal Shalaan males a dime a dozen, and a female a treasure. Your aunt Bahiyah was that for decades. Then came you."

Her hairs stood on end at the way he said those words. It got worse when he leaned closer, and she was hit with another wave of his vigor and virility.

He only placed his empty mug on the floor between them. "It's the one thing that made your family tolerate your Hydra of a mother. That she managed the miracle of giving the Aal Shalaans a female child."

She grimaced. "Hydra, huh? Ouch." Then she laughed. "But, yeah, apt description. Though in anything else, you must be talking about an alternate universe. In this one, I never noticed any tolerance toward my mother. Not that I blame anyone for that. My mother, as you so bluntly noted, *is* intolerable. I also never had any evidence that I was such a big deal to the family for achieving the feat of being born female. In fact, I mostly experienced the opposite. Being the lone estrogen bubble floating in an ocean of testosterone was no fun."

A contemplative look greeted her words. "I expect it must have had its drawbacks."

Her laugh was mirthless this time. "For my first decade I couldn't understand that I wasn't a boy, then I *wouldn't* accept I wasn't, tried my best to be one, so I'd fit in. My mother did her best to flog me, emotionally and sometimes physically, out of my efforts. Then puberty hit and I began to feel some good sides to being a girl." *Like growing a whole new appreciation of his masculine wonder.* "But those did not outweigh the bad. I was such a disappointment to everyone. Not male, so couldn't be shoved into the roles in need of a steady supply of Aal Shalaans, and not the type of female they had in mind. The older I got, the more disgusted with me my mother and aunt became for not inheriting their refined genes, for manifesting the looks and temperament of the Neanderthal-like Aal Shalaans. I was 'tainted' by my Aal Shalaan blood, as my mother put it when she was trying to 'cleanse' me of its disadvantages. And though I cleaned up good when they had their way with me, when left to my own devices, I slipped back into my graceless, disgraceful self. Not that they gave up. They kept hoping that through constant pressure they'd prove the ancient proverb right."

"Which proverb is that?"

"Ekfi'l edrah ala fommaha, tet'la el bent l'ommaha."

"Set the cauldron on its face, after mother the girl takes."

She whooped. "And it almost rhymes, too."

He tutted. "Almost doesn't count. Either it rhymes, or it's lame. That *was* lame."

Another man would have accepted her praise of his translation. He'd accept nothing he hadn't fully earned. The self-made, self-sufficient entity that he was would care nothing about others' approval, anyway.

She waved his dismissal away. "Details. It was good enough. And clever. Not to mention instantaneous."

Not one to continue a subject he'd already dismissed, his gave her what felt like a mind and soul scan. "So your mother and aunt couldn't 'turn' you."

A chuckle overcame her. Yes, he was disparaging her family, but he did it deliciously, not to mention accurately. "Like vampires would, huh? Another spot-on analogy, sorry to admit. And nope. To their escalating frustration, I remained an inferior human with loads of abhorrent failings that made them break out in hives. The worst of it was the traits you had a demonstration of tonight."

Was that teasing that simmered in the blackness of his eyes? Was it even possible?

"Being overriding and unstoppable?"

"Hah. They'd have a stroke if they heard anyone describe me as *that.* Their dissatisfaction with me was based on what they said formed the foundation of my character. In their words, a 'total lack of discretion, insight and shrewdness and a genetic absence of poise, presence and influence.'"

Yep, she'd memorized the slurs. They'd been said in too many variations often enough.

His eyes told her he'd made a note of that fact. "It's clear they didn't know you well."

Her lips relaxed, as did her heart. "Do you mind if I take that as a compliment?"

A perfectly formed hand—strength, skill and command wrapped in bronze and adorned by raven silk—waved her a *knock yourself out*. What she'd give to know those hands better.

She sighed. "Then I began to mess up their plans for me and was exposed to the full measure of their ruthlessness. Just when I thought things couldn't get any worse, their conspiracy to depose Uncle Atef and take over Zohayd was exposed. Not only didn't I see any of it coming, when I was the closest anyone ever got to either of them, I never realized they were capable of such…malevolence. Guess they were right about my lack of insight and shrewdness."

"You feel guilty that you didn't realize what they were planning."

As usual, he was right. "I felt almost responsible. It's one of the main reasons I left Zohayd." She gave a self-deprecating shrug. "And here I am."

"Here you are."

The words hung in the warm air like intoxicating incense. They sounded as if he was glad that she was.

Okay, so a man like Rashid—though there were no men like him—didn't do 'glad.' But there'd been an emotion, as powerful as everything else about him, attached to those three words. Whatever it was, it warmed her, contented her.

Silence enveloped the gigantic space, enfolded them. She soaked up its peace and profundity. She couldn't believe she'd shared with him things she hadn't even told her best friends. How he'd listened, become involved, interested, letting her unburden herself, letting her come closer.

If only he'd reciprocate.

For now he was giving her what she'd never hoped to have.

The pleasure of basking in his nearness and communion, the sense of being isolated with him in a world that contained no one but them. She felt sequestered from everything—the past, the future, existing in a sheer state of presence, in *his* presence.

Then poignancy passed from soul to senses, took hold…and wrenched. The need to smooth her hands down his scar, over that glorious head and shoulders and chest became an ache. But it was the expression on his half-turned face that had tenderness sweeping through her. It was as if he'd forgotten to put on his mask, as if he couldn't hold it in place.

"What are you thinking?" she whispered.

The expression was gone. "Nothing."

"I think it's a fourth impossibility that your mind isn't in high gear every single second you're awake. I bet you're thinking even when you're asleep. It feels as if you're perpetually observing, analyzing, concluding and deciding how to use each and every detail of what's going on around you."

Both eyebrows rose. But he only said, "And the first three impossibilities are?"

"You don't know? But it's a very common saying."

"In Zohayd, I assume. Contrary to common belief, Azmahar was never an extension of Zohayd that splintered into oil-fueled if ill-fated autonomy. It wasn't destined to return to the motherland's bosom begging to be annexed back. Not until ex-king Nedal, that is."

"Whoa. That's a huge nerve you got exposed there. But sheathe your claws, Rashid. I, of all people, don't subscribe to any of that. With said king being my uncle, I'm half-Azmaharian through the side of my family who're responsible for Azmahar's decline. I can do nothing about anyone's actions or what they led to, but I've always loved Azmahar and am proud to call it my second home."

His gaze stilled on her face.

Was that welcome news? Or was he only adjusting another misconception in that fathomless mind of his?

He finally exhaled. "You wouldn't be faulted if you didn't.

Azmahar, as it stands today, doesn't have much to it to love or to be proud of. It was mismanaged and misrepresented by its rulers and constrained and condescended to by its allies for decades. Most of its people have either forgotten what it is to be proud to be Azmaharian, or never learned it was possible to be so."

That urge to touch him, hug him, almost overwhelmed her. "But not you. You're Super Azmahar Man who'll rectify all that, now that you're a candidate for the throne."

His expression changed as if a steel door had slammed shut. It made her realize how much he'd opened up. Another off-limits topic?

When he answered, it seemed she'd imagined all the tension. His shrug was easy. "Candidacy means nothing."

"Only winning does, huh?"

Again he didn't pursue the subject she'd introduced. Which she was burning to know more about.

Since her uncle had been forced to abdicate the throne after a long reign of gross "mismanagement," and his heirs had been rejected for succession, Azmahar had called for a new king. But the country was now divided into three fronts, each supporting a different candidate.

The other two candidates were Haidar and Jalal, her paternal *and* maternal cousins. They'd been dubbed the Princes of Two Kingdoms and so many said they were perfect for the throne of Azmahar.

Which was ridiculous. Though she loved them and they were incredible men and businessmen, she couldn't see how anyone would consider them, or anyone else, when Rashid was in the picture. Apart from being beyond compare as a man, in her own humble opinion, he was full-blooded Azmaharian and a war hero many times over, and the wealthiest, most successful businessman in Azmahar's history.

Rashid's deep-velvet voice interrupted her musings. "You still haven't told me what the first three impossibilities are, according to Zohaydan folklore."

"I do know it's not known in Azmahar, but I thought with

you once spending so much time in Zohayd you'd be as versed as any of us in local colloquial nuances."

"That one must have slipped my omni-awareness."

She couldn't stop herself from laughing out loud. He kept surprising her. That combination of corrosive humor and straight-faced delivery was lethal. Like everything about him. It didn't help to discover he was fun as well as hot as hell. As if she wasn't already in enough trouble.

Feeling as if her smile would never fade, she said, *"Al ghul wal anqa'a wal khell'lel waffi."*

The ghoul, the phoenix and the faithful friend.

His lips curled. "I don't know about the first two but the impossibility of that last one is certain."

That was what he believed? About Haidar and Jalal? The three of them had once been inseparable. More. Bonded beyond even brotherhood. What could have happened to shatter their vital connection?

Dared she ask?

No. She'd stepped on too many of his privacy toes for one night. Something of that magnitude had to be reserved for later.

If there was a later.

With dejection setting in, she sighed. "Both our issues are tied to those who should have been our closest friends."

That again seemed to stun him. "Are you suggesting we have something in common?"

Her astonishment equaled his. "I'm not suggesting. I'm stating."

"It seems more than two years of living in Chicago has dimmed your memory of who you are, princess. And of who I am."

Her eyes rolled. "We're back to princessing me, huh? Please don't tell me you're even suggesting that when it comes to status, I'm the one standing on higher ground!"

"I'm not suggesting. I'm stating."

She almost snorted. "Please! You've overcome unimaginable adversity and are now a phenomenal self-made success story, with a kingdom begging you to be its king. And what am I? While I made enough money to set up my business, and it's beginning to take off, it will never be anywhere near as huge as yours. And while my family might have thought they *were* 'prizing' me—what they actually did was hold me back and almost break me down. I've barely recovered from a lifetime of emotional abuse. At least when your guardian and his family abused you, you had the comfort of knowing they weren't your flesh and blood. So no, there's nothing higher about my status."

Again she felt that vast…wrath percolate inside him. It made her shiver, even when she knew it wasn't directed at her.

"You're still a princess," he finally said.

"A minor one."

"The only daughter of the Aal Shalaans is anything but minor. Your parents are siblings of monarchs. You're next in status only to those in line to the crown of both kingdoms. If that doesn't make you a major princess, I don't know what does."

"Take heart. I'm no longer royal on one side, since my mother's family was ousted from Zohayd and Azmahar. And with Uncle Atef relinquishing Zohayd to Amjad, having only a cousin on the throne distances me from it and diminishes said lofty status."

"Whatever the political developments, you're still royal on both sides going back a few dozen generations."

She threw her hands in the air. "*Ya Ullah*…now I know why dates are *my* fourth impossibility. My statistics make me sound so…stuffy. Not to mention scary. Who wants to go out with a woman with all this ancient blue sludge clogging her veins? And all the minefields that come with it?"

"Any man would do anything to…date you, even if it would jeopardize his very life."

Was *that* a compliment? That doozy? Would "any man" include him? Or was he just saying men would overlook the dangers of associating with her for supposedly unimaginable privileges?

Before she could ask what he meant, he was already asking another question. "You don't date?"

"No." *Because you exist, and any man compared to you is predictable, disappointing and...well, non-existent.* Out loud she qualified her response. "I start nothing I know won't work."

"How do you know it won't work out until you try?"

"One try is enough to tell me it won't."

Ugh. She'd made it sound as if her M.O. was a string of one-night stands, ditching guys who didn't wow her the morning after.

Before she could rectify this massive miscommunication, she found him on his feet.

She blinked up at him. "You gotta teach me how you do that."

An empty glance answered her as he produced his phone. After he again ordered his right hand man to come over, he turned to her.

"It's time you went home, princess."

She found herself on her feet, too, her heart almost uprooting itself in dismay. "But I don't want to go yet."

"It's 1:00 a.m. That woman who seems joined to you at the hip must have already reported you missing."

"Mira had to fly to Tennessee—her father was taken to the emergency room. That's why I haven't called her yet, and why I was going home alone tonight. I was also much later than usual because I had to stay behind and finish things for her."

"So her father forced her into one E.R., and you forced me into another."

Her lips quivered on a mixture of humor and rising anxiety. "As if anyone could force you into anything."

"I once believed no one could. After tonight, I stand corrected. Look what's happened to me since I let that lowlife nick me. I've been dragged to the E.R., pushed into the hands of doctors who had anything but work on their minds, blackmailed back into my car, taken home like a minor, informed how I feel, told to sit and where, and fed and pampered like an invalid. Now I can't even go to bed because you want to fuss over me some more."

No longer sure if he was teasing or fed up, she blurted out, "I promise to stop fussing over you, if you let me stay the night."

And she finally did it. She'd shocked him mute.

When she thought he wouldn't speak again, he exhaled. "Coming here was inappropriate. 'Staying the night' needs new adjectives."

Still not sure what to make of his mood, she ventured a smile. "Unacceptable? Outrageous? Shocking as hell?"

"How about 'out of the question'?"

"C'mon, Rashid, this *is* twenty-first century Chicago."

The hardness settling in his eyes told her no argument would work this time. He'd send her away then tell himself he shouldn't see her again. Tonight was all she could have.

She caught his arm, her voice shaking then breaking. "You can't send me home to an empty condo after what happened tonight."

The frown furrowing his forehead along the lines inflicted by his harsh life was one of bafflement this time. "You're that afraid of being alone? You didn't seem worried before."

"Just because I'm not a mess doesn't mean I'm okay." Which was true. "Only being with you has stopped the whole thing from sinking in and ripping at my insides." Which was also true.

His eyes widened that fraction that told her something major was going on inside him. This was the moment she had to seize, when he was teetering on the verge of relenting, before he talked himself out of softening.

She did. "Let me stay with you. Please, Rashid."

Her insides were quivering for his verdict when he suddenly let out a long breath.

Before she could gauge if that was exasperation or capitulation, he turned and walked away.

As she struggled with worry, he threw her a cool glance over his shoulder. "One thing for sure, princess. Your mother and aunt were clueless about you. You could influence the dead."

She hurried after him, needing confirmation. "And since you're very much alive, this means I can stay?"

"At your peril, princess."

Five

Talk about false advertisement.

Despite Rashid's thrilling warning about her spending the night, nothing had happened.

In fact, what she'd feared most had occurred. He'd treated her like an inapproachable charge in his custody.

This gigantic residence turned out to have separate areas, even though none had any doors since the place was made for one person's privacy. One area was in the mezzanine, behind a partitioning wall, which was used as his bedroom suite. This was the space he'd given her for the night.

The huge room was even sparser than the rest of the place, with only a skylight, a built-in wardrobe and a nine-by-nine-foot mattress spread in dark sheets on the floor. But to her delight, the connecting bathroom was decadent. It was good to know that although his living and sleeping quarters were a throw-back to his life as a survivalist, where hygiene was involved, Rashid had succumbed to state-of-the-art luxury.

He'd offered her some of his clean clothes to wear. But since he had nothing to replace her stilettos, he'd encouraged her to go barefoot, assuring her he kept the floors spotless. Then, without so much as a good-night, he'd left her.

And here she was, sitting on his "bed," flooded to the knee in his sweatshirt and unable to sleep.

Not because he'd let her stay the night with him, but not really with him at all. But because now that she'd had time to think, she realized the real reason behind her earlier desperation to stay. She'd sensed something was very wrong. With him.

She *had* felt it, heard it and seen it while he'd been ripping her attackers apart. That volcanic rage that had incinerated his reason. Far beyond anything an ordinary man would feel about scum who preyed on a helpless female. Something uncontrollable, consuming. Damaging. Terrible.

The effort she'd felt him exert to bring his violence under control, the volatility she'd felt him struggle with so he could appear stable under her scrutiny, had singed her with its intensity. This hadn't been a new reaction ignited by tonight's events. This was old. And immense. She could not begin to imagine what had spawned it. But she knew whatever it was continued to prey on him. That demon she'd felt possessing him, body and mind, was just beneath the surface.

And even before she'd analyzed all that consciously, she hadn't been able to let that demon consume the man she loved any further, not when it *had* manifested in full force this time on her account.

Oh, yes. Love. There was no use calling what she felt for him anything else.

So what if he was no longer the same man she'd had a crush on all her life? He was now far more than anything she'd ever imagined. Darker, larger-than-life, more complex and intriguing than anyone she'd ever met. Even under normal circumstances, she would have been disturbed at the prospect of allowing herself any emotional involvement with this highly upgraded Rashid. But she saw no reason for caution or trepidation now when she never had before. She wouldn't have to deal with the consequences of emotions that would no doubt remain unrequited. Rashid was driven, self-contained and off-limits. He had no place in his life for a woman or in his heart for love.

But it didn't matter. It brought her peace to accept her emotions, even revel in them. To know the one man she could love existed, and why exactly she loved him, and would never be with another.

It wasn't as pathetic or melodramatic as it sounded. She'd even call it wise, since *that* was learning from others' experiences and mistakes. She'd seen too many marriages that had been made without love and how disastrously they'd ended, or worse, continued. She also had the example of those marriages that had flourished because they'd been based on the kind of love that came once in a lifetime, and thrived against all odds. *That* kind of love she'd feel only for Rashid. It was unwise, even self-destructive, settling for less. But what were the odds he'd reciprocate her emotions? Negligible, really.

He might have let her "influence" him tonight, but only as an extension of his chivalry. Maybe the old times he'd discounted did count for a man afflicted by a gargantuan sense of honor. After all, he'd once gone to unimaginable lengths to pay the debts of a man who'd abused him, to repay that man for the shelter he'd given him when the already motherless Rashid had become a complete orphan.

Suddenly, that familiar chill moved through her.

She now knew the feeling was a Rashid proximity alert. Could he be approaching? If he was, would it be because he...?

She wished. He must be coming to check up on her after she'd misled him about the nature of her turmoil. But what if...

Reality check, moron. He probably just wanted something from the bedroom she occupied.

Breath bated, she expected him to walk in any moment.

He didn't. Had she imagined it?

No. Something had intensified her awareness of him. This might mean... Something was wrong!

Who knew where that scumbag's switchblade had been?

That wound Rashid had dismissed might be starting to fester. He'd probably refused antibiotics like he had analgesics.

She shot to her feet. At the mezzanine's railing, her streak came to a stumbling halt as if she'd slammed into an invisible force field. From the far end of the hangar-sized space, something reverberated in her ears, her bones. It felt and sounded like the erratic, furious pounding of a distant, gigantic heart.

She hadn't heard the sound in the sequestered bedroom area. But it must have been what had sent anxiety skewering through her.

She ran down the stairs, almost slipping on the slick stone. Once her feet touched rougher floor, her dash resumed. The force of the sounds ratcheted up with every step as she approached a wall partition at the far end of the loft. Beyond it, the pounding felt as if it would bruise her insides.

Her own heart thundering in response, she walked around the wall. And she saw the sound's origin. *Rashid.*

Stripped to the waist, barefoot and barehanded, he was kickboxing a punching bag in a constant barrage of viciousness that had almost destroyed its supposedly indestructible form. Those punches and roundhouse kicks could bring down a wall. A single one would have killed anything living. It made her realize he'd actually held back when he'd dealt with her attackers.

It was as if he was venting surplus anger, tearing the bag apart as he hadn't a chance to do to them. Or was he imagining striking out at those who'd given him his ghastly scar?

Ya Ullah—that *scar.*

Continuing on a path of mutilation from his neck, it widened as it ran down his back. At his waist it snaked around to his front, as if to shackle his body, slithered up over his abdomen to his chest in a passage of livid disfiguration. Where it ended, its very tip, sharp and jagged, seemed to plunge beneath his skin to skewer into his heart.

It certainly felt as if it had plunged into hers. What he must have suffered!

B'Ellahi—how and when had this happened to him? And

more important, what had it done to him? How deeply had that scar sunk into his psyche, into his soul?

It sank talons of anguish into hers.

Yet as she neared, fascination began to replace the anguish that gripped her insides. He was moving so fast, she hadn't been able to make out what that darkness staining his skin around the scar was. She'd at first thought it was charred flesh, making her almost want to retch. But now she realized what it was.

A tattoo. Weaving around the scar as if to ward off its advance, stop it from spreading its damage.

Then she was close enough to fathom its complex configuration, to realize what the shapes enveloping the scar were. An ingenious pattern made of the symbol of the noble house he belonged to, a distant branch of her maternal family, of which he was the last surviving member.

She stood for what felt like hours, mesmerized, watching that powerhouse display of heart-wrenching rage and mind-numbing might. His skin, flawless apart from the scar that marred it and that he'd so boldly outlined, glowed as if real flames fueled his fury. Sweat accentuated the polish and definition of every formidable muscle, spraying crystalline droplets with each swing. His every line and move was sheer poetry of power and perfection.

What kind of training and drive fueled this level of expertise and endurance? He didn't even seem to be breathing hard. Or seem to show that he'd ever slow down or stop.

Suddenly, he did, his arms falling to his sides. Fists clenched, he remained rock-still, feet planted apart, primed for reeruption into full-blown aggression, staring at his handiwork, every muscle bunched on the precarious control that momentarily contained the demon driving him to such excesses.

She'd never seen anything so absolutely magnificent.

Even unaware of her presence, lost to his inner struggle, his aura flooded her. It felt mystical, limitless. A knight with might enough to bear mythical burdens, determination enough to forge legends. She had no doubt she was looking at the only man who could restore Azmahar to its now-distant glory. He might have lived as an orphan and an outcast, but he was born to be a king.

He'd always been king of her heart.

And she couldn't bear witnessing his turmoil. He'd suffered enough. She'd give anything so he wouldn't suffer ever again.

"Rashid."

At her tremulous whisper, he swung around, his face a mask of surprise, his slanting eyes widening, the flames beneath his skin blazing brighter.

"Laylah…"

It was the first time he'd ever said her name. *Just* her name.

Hearing it in that incomparable voice of his, darkness and magic made audible, shot liquid fire from her heart to flood her limbs. Her feet almost tangled around each other as she approached him. The field of agitation enveloping them tightened, choking her as she stopped before him.

Surprise deserted his face, harshness replacing it, hardening its hewn angles. "Don't you know curiosity always backfires, princess? Now you have to live with this sight polluting your mind's eye forever."

Her gaze darted to where his exercise pants hung precariously low on his muscled hips. She forced it back up to his drenched face. "Your all-out revenge on the punching bag?"

Those obsidian flames lashed out from his eyes again. "Are you pretending that this—" he made a sweeping gesture to his tattooed scar "—doesn't horrify you? I thought you had enough courage and candor to spare me the damned political correctness. Everyone struggles to pretend my scar doesn't exist, when it's all anyone can see anymore, and they're torn between cringing, curiosity and the unreasoning worry that it will somehow infect them. But to a perfect woman used to perfection in everything, especially in men, I know it must revolt you, princess."

"Rev—?" That zapped any languidness his nearness provoked. "Now listen here, *Sheikh* Rashid. I've put up with you misconceptions, since I realized you know nothing about me, and I was willing to educate you. But this is where I won't try to convince you. This is where I'll *tell* you." She grabbed his arms, stood on tiptoes, to make up for the disadvantage of being dwarfed by him and his sweatshirt, to inject her posture with authority. "*You* have always defined perfection to me."

His eyes shot wider, as if she'd punched him in the gut.

Shocked? How much more shocked would he be when she touched him where his flesh had been sundered and sealed along that terrible rift?

Her hand trembled as it fulfilled her overwhelming need.

It stopped midway, caught in the iron vise of his hand.

Raising her eyes, she found his face gripped with a ferociousness that would have scared off anyone else.

It only made touching him a necessity. Her heart felt it would stop if she didn't.

Her other hand rose, met with the same fate, made her almost whimper. "Please, Rashid. Let me touch you."

"Why? Even if I believed your wild claim, my alleged perfection is a thing of the past, from before I was almost torn apart and so sloppily put back together. So don't you dare placate or pity me. I don't take kindly to either offense."

This needed taking care of, once and for all.

Hands gripped in his, she forced her lips to quiver into a smile. "Fine. Just remember, I tried to spare you. You now have only yourself to blame when I give you my uncensored opinion."

His hands convulsed around hers before he let them go. Then, face empty of expression, he stepped back.

Her heart twisted. It was as if he needed to hear it from a safe distance. He believed her true opinion would hurt.

She bridged the distance he'd put between them, taking his hands, insisting on keeping him in place. "When you were younger and softer and in one pristine piece, you more than defined perfection for me. You filled my 'mind's eye' with your impossible example and made anyone else fade into nothing."

She clung to his hands harder when he again attempted to jerk them away. "But that scar, what you've been through to have it, only to come out stronger—how you wear it as a tribute to your family and ancestors, making it the very embodiment of your noble house—it makes you indescribable. And infinitely more irresistible."

Judging that the time to reach out again was now, when she had him boggling at the audacity of her confessions, her hands released his, making another attempt to reach his scar.

His hands caught them before she could blink. "You can't really want to touch…this."

"Did *indescribable* and *irresistible* have too many syllables for you to understand? I would find you both even if you were scarred all over. I don't only *want* to touch you, I've been waiting all my *life* to do it."

This time, his stupefaction was almost tangible.

Pouncing on the opening it afforded her, she persisted, "Will you let me touch you? Please?"

A full-scale war seemed to erupt within him.

Then, with his gaze the darkest it had ever been, he let go of her hands.

Her first instinct was to pounce on him. But that starving-woman-at-a-buffet routine would be too much for him at this point.

Instead, she reached out, hands trembling as they made that first contact. With the scar at his heart.

The moment her flesh met his at that mark of old and severe pain and damage, her whole being seized, as if her essence flowed through her fingertips into him. She would give endlessly of it, if it would only erase his suffering, past and present.

On the verge of breaking down, her voice wobbled on the question that seared her. "Does— Does it still hurt?"

"No."

The monosyllable conveyed how much and how long it *had* hurt.

"What does it feel like?"

A shudder coursed through him. Or it might be she who was shaking so hard. She couldn't tell where the tremors originated.

"People stop asking when they know it's not painful anymore." His voice was thicker, impeded. "They don't think any other sensation but pain matters."

Empathy tightened her throat. "I'm not people. I'm me. And anything that you feel matters to me. Matters, period." Unable to hold back anymore, one hand curled around his nape, urging his head down so her lips could follow her fingers in exploring that scar that made her only far more appreciative and protective of his every other inch. This time, there was no mistaking the jolt that passed through him as her lips traveled from the edge of his jaw down to the root of his powerful neck. She held him closer, insistent against his damp, hot skin. "Tell me, Rashid."

Letting her discover every inch of his scar, his voice ragged, he said, "If I'm totally still, I can convince myself it doesn't exist. But at the slightest movement, it feels as if the ruined skin no longer belongs to me. It sometimes feels like a chasm into another reality, a fault line where something malicious seeps into my body, infects me with its poison."

So he *did* feel possessed. She'd do whatever it took to make sure he didn't feel that way ever again.

Slipping around him, her lips followed the scar as it flowed from his neck to his back, as if she *would* kiss it better, suck all the negative energy into herself.

"How do you feel when it's touched?" she whispered.

She felt his tension spike before it resumed buzzing through him like high voltage through a maximum-resistance cable. His voice was a hoarse rasp when he answered. "The few times it was touched, it felt like a jolt of acute discomfort and revulsion. It made me feel…violent."

Her lips stopped over his shoulder blade, along with her heart. "Do— Do you feel like that now?"

"No."

Her heart clanged at his instantaneous negation.

When he didn't qualify it, she resumed her exploration, bolder now. "Then how do you feel when I do this…?"

A finger joined her lips in their sweep through the ridge.

When nothing but his slow, deep breathing answered her— which to the über-fit Rashid constituted panting—she nudged her head against his arm. He raised it, letting her follow an uninterrupted path up his abdomen to where the scar ended over his heart.

At the very tip, she slipped her tongue out to taste it and him. The voltage coursing through him almost electrocuted her.

She raised her gaze, panting. "How does that feel, Rashid?"

His face looked like a force of nature roused. His voice did sound like muted thunder when he answered. "Your every touch, your every breath triggers everything I can feel at once. It's as if every sensation is amplified within the scar's confines only to shoot out to my every nerve ending."

Her hands stilled over the scar's tip as she wet lips so dry she felt they'd crack. "Sounds…distressing."

He followed her tongue's movements, something deliciously scary smoldering in his eyes. "It is. Overwhelmingly so. It's pleasurable to the point of pain. And arousing to beyond madness."

His fingers were suddenly digging into her hair, twisting into her long tresses, tilting her face up to his. Her lips opened on a gasp of shock and pleasure at the spikes that shot from every hair to her toes, pooling in between in her core in a heavy, liquid throb.

She swayed into him, feeling the sensual whirlpool he generated tugging her under. At the touch of her length against his, his steady grip trembled once before firming again.

Holding her eyes, he singed her with intensity. "Is this what you want me to feel, princess? Is this what you want me to do?"

And his lips crashed over hers.

At the impact of his passion, a cry burst from her, laden with surprise, relief, delight and a dozen other emotions. He swallowed it, poured his own groans into her. Her lips opened wider, begging for more of his taste and ferocity.

She needed this kiss, this man she'd been waiting for all her life, more than she needed her next breath.

"Is this what you want?" He tore his lips away from hers to growl against her cheeks, her forehead, her neck, roaming over her with demand, owning her. At her frantic nod, he swept up the sweatshirt he'd loaned her, cupped her buttocks in the warmth of his large, calloused hands. Pressing her against the wall, he opened her thighs, grinding against her core with the massive hardness his pants barely contained. "Is this what you've been after as you pushed me and pulled at me and exposed me to your inexorable temptation? Do you want me to lose every shred of restraint, every spark of sanity and devour you whole?"

He accentuated his last words by thrusting against her in an explicit mimicking of possession. She could only moan her consent, going limp in his arms.

"Be absolutely sure it's what you want, princess. I would have taken nothing, but if you say yes, I'll take it all."

Was he trying to scare her off? For her own good?

She had to convince him her only "good" was to be with him.

She struggled to wrap her legs around his hips, but was quaking so much, her legs slipped off him. She moaned in thankfulness when he scooped them up and held them around him.

Her hands trembled over his head as she transmitted her conviction into his eyes. "I am an all-or-nothing kind of person myself. And make no mistake, Rashid, I want it all with you."

He pressed harder into her, as if testing her claims. "*You* make no mistake, give me one more intimacy and I'll take everything you have. *Everything*, princess."

The misguided man still thought the idea of his ravishing her could scare her away.

She decided to stoke all that ferocity higher. "You mean if at any point I say stop, you won't?"

His eyes blazed in imperious confidence. "You will not want me to stop."

She dragged his head down to hers, opened her lips over his scar, grazed it with her teeth. "Yet here I am still trying to convince you to start—"

She trailed off on a yelp. In another of those magical moves, he swept her up in his arms.

She snuggled against his muscled shoulder, soaking up the momentous feeling. He was striding across his domain, taking her to where she'd thought she'd spend the night alone then leave to never see him again. Could it be that everything she'd ever dreamed of was coming true instead? She would finally be with Rashid?

Her fingers dug into his arm, making him slow down. "I want *you* to be clear on something, Rashid." He smoldered down at her, awaiting her conditions. "You will give me everything, too."

After a protracted, unreadable glance, he gave a brief nod.

He accepted her terms, would abide by them.

Elation fizzed in her blood even as arousal thickened it.

And that was before he said, "Just remember, when I give you everything, it was you who asked for it."

Promises, promises, she almost said.

But teasing Rashid would come later. When he opened up to her more. Hopefully soon. And fully.

For now, she would take one miracle at a time.

Six

The miracle wasn't unfolding as Laylah had anticipated.

It had played to her expectations till Rashid had lowered her onto his bed. Then it had diverged onto a totally unexpected path.

Instead of continuing his seduction, he'd risen to his feet. He now stood brooding down at her.

"Rashid, *arjook*..."

Was that her voice? That thick, covetous rasp?

But who could blame her? The man she'd fantasized about all her life was standing before her, proving her most extravagant fantasies of him modest.

Instead of answering her plea, he was turning away, tossing words over his shoulder. "You won't appreciate me all over you sweaty like this." Before she could cry out that she *loved* him sweaty like that, would want him all over her even slathered in mud, he dragged his blunt fingernails down his face, producing a scratching sound that deluged her in a fresh bout of tremors. "I've also grown some industrial strength sandpaper."

Next second, he disappeared into the bathroom.

* * *

The moment he closed the bathroom door, Rashid bolted
into the shower, turned it on cold and plunged beneath its freezing spray.

Gulping down air, he squeezed his eyes shut, leaned his
flaming forehead against the cold tiles, willing the icy needles
to pummel arousal's hold on his senses.

What was he *doing?*

This had progressed so fast. Too fast. Too far.

Even when he'd been doing everything in his power to sabotage his own plans, it had only accelerated them.

Now she was out there, the woman he'd meant to eventually
have in his bed, begging him to take her, now, not later. When
he hadn't done a thing to seduce her, had done the opposite
trying to ward her away, giving her every reason to back off.

It would have been an ingenious strategy had he meant it
pulling away so she'd be the one to pursue him, but he'd genu-
inely tried everything he could to dissuade her.

Now that he'd failed, he couldn't go through with it. For she
wasn't the woman he'd meant to seduce. *That* woman existed
only in his preconceptions. The real Laylah was something
he hadn't known existed. A being pure of heart and magnanimous. And she wasn't seeking him in response to a maddening challenge.

She truly wanted him. And had for all her life, she'd said.

He shouldn't have let her touch him.

Her hands and lips on his disfigured flesh had… *Ya Ullah*..

He'd never known there could be sensations like that. They'
bolted from his flesh to his psyche, tearing into him, detonating
his barriers, his brakes. Nothing had mattered after that firs
touch but that she kept on touching him. As she had.

Then she'd told him she wanted it all with him. He had
no idea how he'd stopped himself from dragging her to the
ground right then and there and driving inside her, assuaging
their mutual need.

But he couldn't take what she was so fervently offering. No

after the past hours' experiences and revelations. Not now that he knew she wasn't who he'd thought she was.

He now owed her far better than that.

Yet how could he deny her, after he'd promised her himself?

He would give her one last chance to make sure. If being with him in ultimate intimacy was as necessary to her as it was to him, and not a reaction to tonight's turmoil, he'd have to succumb.

Laylah stared at the bathroom door, worry preying on her.

When the door finally opened, it felt like it had been ten hours instead of just ten minutes. The scent of the musky soap she'd used earlier preceded Rashid. Bonded to his own scent, it smelled different, intoxicating. The flames that hadn't dimmed in his absence roared higher.

What if her absence had doused his? What would she do?

But…what was she *doing,* asking him to do…*this?*

Her fantasies had never taken her so far. They'd been so tentative that the most they'd dared contemplate was a kiss. Now…this.

Did she even have any idea what *this* would be like? What it would lead to? Or wouldn't lead to? Was this how she wanted to have him? Because she'd thrown herself at him until he couldn't resist anymore?

He came to stand over her again. Clean-shaven, head and skin still gleaming with wetness, his beauty twisted a spear of longing through her gut. She leaned limply against the wall, her legs tucked beneath her, hands folded over her heart, as if to stop it from beating its way out of her chest.

He finally murmured, "Your beauty is incomparable." She gaped at him. "But this must have been the first thing you learned about yourself, princess."

She'd learned no such thing. Not that she was about to debate it. If he thought so, even if it turned out he only needed glasses, she wouldn't jar him from his illusion.

"I could see your potential from the time you were six. I

knew your beauty would become so overpowering, men would fight over you and kings would fall at your feet. I was right. The list of the royals who have begged for your hand is as tall as you are."

She cast a deprecating glance down her body. While not short, she was the shortest in her family at five foot six. "Not really tall, with a sum total of seven such 'royals.' And none was after my 'overpowering beauty' but rather my 'overwhelming connections.'"

"If that was true, then the only explanation is that they're not into women. What heterosexual male would not want you?"

"Uh…off the top of my head, I know of eighty-eight such males."

He shook his head. "Your relatives don't count."

But she hadn't counted as a desirable female to any man that she knew of. Whatever her personal assets, they'd always been nullified by her family's. Men had either wanted her, or hadn't wanted her, based on those. Not that she'd ever cared. Not when Rashid was the only man she'd ever wanted.

His gaze, sliding from the feet tucked beneath her to her face, felt like a full-body caress. "It almost…hurts to look at you."

Her smile wavered. "I'm hoping that's a compliment."

"It's the truth." He was suddenly on his knees, facing her on the mattress. "You're an impossibility. I don't believe in perfection, but here you are, against everything I believe. And against anything I *can* believe, you say you want me."

Her heart kicked so hard it brought her up on her knees, too, looking fervently up at him. "I *do* want you. I always have."

The brooding look gripping his face deepened. "You said I defined perfection to you. So now I ask—how? What is it about me that you ever found perfect, let alone now?"

A drop of water streaked down his chest and caught in the groove of his scar, making her tongue ache to lick it off.

She dragged her gaze up to his. "It would be easier to count the things I don't find perfect about you. Like how you were always so distant, as if in a world of your own. But then, that's not an imperfection, just a frustration." Giving in to the need, her fingertips swept a trembling path down his scar. "The thing is, you might not be perfect per se. But you are perfect to me."

A large hand covered hers, pressed it to his six pack of steel. "I had time to reconsider in the shower."

Oh, no! He'd say he'd lost his head under her temptation, reprimand her for being inappropriate again and end this. Then in the morning she'd leave and never find her way back to him again.

But she'd taken this as far as she could. Anything he decided now, she had to abide by.

She waited for his verdict, her teeth starting to chatter.

His eyebrows furrowed as he documented her reaction. "Whatever I said before, you must not think it's too late to change your mind. You're free to reconsider."

The letdown felt like the two-floors'-worth fall from this mezzanine onto the stone ground below.

She gritted her teeth on a sob that almost escaped, forced steadiness in her voice. "If you want to take back everything you said, *you* feel free. You don't have to let me down easy."

His eyes narrowed. "You mean you still feel the same way?"

Her shoulders slumped. "It's not important what I feel."

"It's all-important. But what you feel now could be PTS."

"Post-traumatic stress? From the attack, you mean?"

"It's common to need to reaffirm life through uncharacteristic, uninhibited acts after surviving a life-threatening experience."

"And you're an expert in that, right?" His gaze dropped, his whole face becoming inanimate. Beyond trying to analyze his reaction, she had to resolve this. "Since I detailed my lifelong crush on you, you know this isn't spur of the moment on my part. If you want to give me a way out of looking like a pathetic fool by pretending it was the stress talking, go ahead, be chivalrous to the end."

Without raising his eyes, he murmured, "The last thing I am is chivalrous."

She sagged back on her heels. "Then it's even worse. You succumbed to an 'uncharacteristic and uninhibited act' because *you're* stressed and had a hormonal surge due to a woman throwing herself at you and pawing you all over. Now that the urge has subsided, you want to end this on a not-too-sour note."

His eyes rose then, bored into hers again. "Does it look like my 'hormonal surge' has subsided?" His gaze lowered, dragging hers with it and... *Whoa*. His clean sweatpants showed that...nothing had subsided. Not in the least. "And women have thrown themselves at me and pawed me before, and none has caused even a hormonal blip."

Her heart thundered. "You mean you still want...want..."

Desire surged in his voice and gaze again. "Everything. But I needed to be sure I wouldn't be taking advantage of your vulnerability."

So. Moment of truth. Setting him, and herself, straight. She wanted everything with him, whatever it led to.

She leaned into him, spread her hands over his formidable chest, moaning at feeling his vitality and power quiver beneath her touch. "If another man had saved me tonight, I would have made sure he got medical attention and promised to be there for him if he ever needed my help. But I wouldn't have gone home with him, and I certainly wouldn't be in his bed now. From the E.R. onward, everything I did was because it was you. Everything I feel is for you. All I want is *you*."

He suddenly severed their contact by standing up.

At her choking disappointment, he said, "To do your unrepeatable offer of everything justice, I've revised my approach of gulping you down whole."

Biting her lip on the yo-yoing agitation and excitement, she whispered, "So what will you do?"

He undid the drawstrings of his pants ever so slowly. "I'll savor you within an inch of your sanity."

She wanted to tell him she was already a few miles beyond sane. That when he let those pants drop, she might suffer a coronary. Then he did.

Finding black silk boxers beneath didn't ward off the mini heart attack. The potency tenting it, those muscled thighs and legs encased in the perfect amount of black silk, and imagining what all that would soon be doing to her, was enough.

Then, muscles rippling, he knelt before her again. He skimmed his lips over her face and neck, inhaling her, groaning his delight at her scent. The conqueror she'd expected him to be had turned into a seducer bound on driving her out of her mind.

Tears stung her eyes as she tried to wind herself around him. "Don't savor me, Rashid. *Arjook,* I can't wait…"

He gently disentangled himself, groaned deep inside her mouth, "Don't rush me, *ya ameerati.* Let me do all this beauty and generosity justice."

It was only that she realized he was in as much torment as she was, that made her concede and suffer his pace.

His hands trembled as he released her from the few clothes she had on, which though loose had become suffocating. She writhed and moaned, caressing his head, drawing him closer, wishing there was hair for her hands to convulse in. At the first touch of those electrifying hands on her breasts, she scraped her fingernails across his scalp. He groaned in equal suffering, but wouldn't hurry.

By the time he had her naked, she knew what erotic torment truly was. It was still worth it, just to see his face as he looked down at her.

She cried out at the savage hunger in his eyes. He closed them instantly, opened them again with it under control. Still afraid for her alleged fragile state of mind?

But he couldn't control the raggedness in his voice. "*Anti akthar menn kamelah*—more than perfect. You're beauty incarnate."

Her head thrashed in protest. "That would be you."

He caught it in gentle hands, pressed a fierce kiss on her lips. "You honor me with your approval, but let me show you how much I hunger for every inch of you…"

And he showed her. He drank her lips dry, then moved to her neck, her arms, her hands. When he drew one of her fingers inside his hot mouth, pleasure forked through her, lodging deep into her core. She hadn't *known* that it could be like this. That he could do this to her, just sucking a finger. Then his lips pulled—hard.

She bucked off the mattress. The throb between her legs squeezed another rush of molten agony. *"Rashid...arjook, daheenah..."*

She was coming apart, needed him now...*now*...

But he had other plans, deeper levels of torment. He exposed her to all forms of sensual stimulation, plumbing every response she hadn't known her body was equipped with, taking every intimacy as he'd warned, creating erogenous zones wherever his hands and lips landed, or his tongue and teeth followed.

He was everywhere. Kneading, kissing, licking. Nibbling, nipping and suckling. Her feet, down her back, all over her stomach and breasts and buttocks, the insides of her arms and thighs. All the time coming up to plunge deeper and deeper kisses into her mouth, along with more aroused, arousing confessions. She lost count how many times she begged for him.

When he finally drew away, she thought he'd at last remove the only remaining barrier between them and join his body with hers. She rose to hurry him, welcome him...

Next second she was flat on her back with her legs over his shoulders. Surprise and consternation warred inside her as a wave of contrary shyness overtook her. She'd been begging to share the ultimate intimacy with him, but had qualms about letting him have a lesser one? Stupid, but no less cripplingly real.

Panting, she tried to sit up. "I want you, Rashid, *you*..."

"You'll have me, all of me. But first I feast on all of you."

He drew her legs wider apart, flattened on his stomach between them, cupping her buttocks, opening her core fully to him. Before one more neuron could fire, he blew a hot breath on the knot where it felt every last nerve in her body converged.

The sound that she made was one of alien hunger. Coherence

seeped out of her, nothing remaining but craving and sensation. The emptiness inside her was spreading, engulfing her...

Her head thrashed, her face tangled in her hair. "You're killing me..."

"I'm worshiping you, *ya ajmal an'naas.*"

Hearing him call her "my princess" before, not just princess was one thing. But "most beautiful of all people"? That he thought such a thing, the way he said it, only made her state more acute. Then he slid a rough, careful finger between the molten lips of her core.

She screamed, bowed up, her whole body quaking. Her breathing stopped, her heartbeat stumbled.

One trembling but insistent hand soothed her down, kneading her breasts, rolling her nipples as his other hand stroked her liquefied flesh in tight circles, just the right speed, just the perfect pressure. She writhed and begged for him more and more. He only quickened his ministrations, and quakes started, radiating from where his fingers played her flesh like a virtuoso. Her hips undulated, moving with his fingers, ripples of delight hurtling with frightening speed toward something far more intense than she'd ever felt or imagined...

He rubbed his now-smooth face against her tender inner thighs, like a lion nuzzling his mate. He sounded like one when he growled, "So hot and fragrant, so ready for me. Now to taste you..."

A shriek tore out of her at his tongue's first plunge into her, drinking her pleasure at the source. Tightening his hold over her bucking buttocks, he swept its firm, slick heat through her trembling flesh to the pinpoint of torment. She imploded, collapsing back on herself.

Then he sucked her flesh into his mouth, unleashing every spark of accumulated sensation.

She ceased to exist, dissipated in wave after wave of white-hot release...

The shudders racking her finally eased, her vision returned

to the sight of his regal head between her thighs, still suckling her, drawing out her aftermath.

Closing her eyes, she melted back into his cossetting, surrendered to his ministrations.

Suddenly, her eyes snapped open. Pleasure wasn't subsiding, it was building, the screaming tension for release back in full force. He went on and on until she was heaving and keening again, in the merciless grip of an even fiercer climax.

Afterward, inside a body that was no longer hers to command and a mind she felt she had no access to, she saw him rise to prowl over her numb body, sweeping her with soothing caresses. Her eyes stung again at his generosity, his restraint. She couldn't believe a man could deny himself so long when he was as agonizingly aroused as Rashid evidently was.

But instead of moving on top of her, he tugged her into the curve of his great body, stroking her quivering flesh gently, murmuring praise and passion in that voice that spoke to her soul.

"Laylah…the taste and sight and sound of your pleasure, everything about you—is beyond perfect, beyond belief…"

What was beyond belief was that he was arousing her again, when she suspected he was trying to lull her to sleep, too. When she'd thought he'd drained her of sensation, maybe forever. Now that her body knew what kind of pleasure he could provide, his merest touch and breath had it clawing its demand for his.

She twisted in his arms, wound herself around him, arms and legs. "You promised me yourself."

Something almost frightening erupted in his eyes. His voice couldn't hide his state, either. "Don't pour more fuel on the fire now, *ya ameerati*."

"I will if it's the only way you're going to stop worshipping me and give me what I need—you, inside me." Catching his face between her hands, she rained kisses all over it before sliding to his scar, suckling and nibbling it in abandon, moaning against his burning flesh, "Come inside me, Rashid, *arjook*. I feel my heart will stop if you don't fill me…now, Rashid, *now!*"

Those roughened hands whose touch drove her out of her mind and ignited every last one of her senses, tightened on her arms as he turned her on her back, loomed over her.

"My condition is reversed. My heart beats thirty beats a minute." Wow. Now *that* was fitness! "At maximum exertion it reaches seventy. Feel it now." He clasped her trembling hand to the pulse point below his scar. The artery leaping beneath her touch was doing so at much higher than seventy beats a minute. "That's what needing to be inside you is doing to me. Holding back is taxing my system more than the toughest survival test."

Her teeth caught at his magnificent cleft chin and nipped. "Serves you right for holding out on me."

His lips twitched as he repaid her nip with a nibble that traveled down to her breast. By the time he was suckling one nipple with his fingers tormenting the other, she had tears of arousal pouring down her cheeks.

She dug discharging fingers into his shoulders. "You misunderstood my condition. It's the same as yours. My heart will stop because it will run out of beats."

Obeying her desperation at last, he rose above her, caressed the thighs that spread in eagerness for him.

Moving between them, he leaned his daunting bulk over her. "I *will* stop your heart. With pleasure."

His sandpaper growl made her swoon, and her hands fumbled with his boxers, needing this last barrier out of the way. His lips tugged in approval of her frenzy, letting her free him. But her hands lost all coordination the moment she released what she'd been begging for. The sheer beauty and size of him was…was…

Her core clenched with intimidation, only to flood in a surplus of readiness.

All she could do now was lie there, open, panting, need tearing at her. "*Arjook,* Rashid, *arjook…*"

And still he didn't plunge inside her. Holding her gaze with an intensity she felt would singe her retinas, he groaned, "Look at me, at us. Look what I'm going to do to you."

His gaze lowered, taking hers with it to where he held his shaft in his hand. Then he leaned, put the head of his erection to her engorged folds. She cried out at the sensation, her back bowing in a steeper arch of surrender, her core opening to him in total offering.

Growling something indiscernible, one of his hands secured her buttocks while the other moved his shaft against her flesh, bathing himself in her desire. At each nudge, sensations shredded through her, tightening the coil of desperation more with every grind.

Soon he had her on the edge of unraveling again, almost but not quite breaching her. She keened, her undulations fevered, her breathing fractured, her frenzy complete.

Then, holding her by her tresses and by his tempestuous gaze, he growled, "Now look—at us, as I take you, as you take me."

The moment she obeyed, he slid inside her.

The power of his thrust forged through her barrier, tore it apart, before his shaft stabbed past into the depths that yielded for him.

A scream welled somewhere deep within her, but it couldn't pummel through the barricade of total shock to her system, to her soul. Everything inside her converged on the part of him that was embedded in her depths like a red-hot lance.

Time stretched before blindness started to part. Harsh breathing, inside her, around her, filling her ears. Her reigniting vision filled with his face. Dark, frozen. His body was bunched over her, still. His eyes ferocious in their focus, unreadable.

But the pain was retreating like a rushing out tide. In its place an unbelievable feeling of fullness was taking over her, an unknown mindlessness rushing in. Her body knew what it wanted. For him to *move*. To fill her over and over and assuage that maddening ache.

But he didn't move. His gaze bored into hers until she almost screamed, this time in frustration. Why wasn't he moving?

"You should have told me."

Her teeth clattered at the way he said it. At the realization that she hadn't told him she was—had been—a virgin. She'd been so far out of her mind that she hadn't considered that fact. Hadn't realized that was why his invasion had felt like it had ripped her apart until he'd brought it to her attention.

What did he feel about it? Concerned? Worried? Angry? Would he have taken her had he known? Would he stop now?

It was next to impossible to think of anything but being overstretched with his potency, invaded, delirious with the carnality, with the completion. She felt she'd die if he withdrew.

Then he was withdrawing, making her claw at him. "Rashid...don't leave...don't stop...*arjook*—give me..."

When he hesitated, her legs clamped around him, pulling him back into her deepest reaches. This time the cry that escaped her was one of exultation, of ecstasy.

She'd thought he'd filled her on that first thrust. He now felt as if he'd never hit bottom, as if he'd forged all the way inside her to her womb, to her heart. She trembled all over, inside and out, as if with the advance tremors of a major quake.

She arched into him, begging for what would unleash the sensations that would disintegrate her if they accumulated more.

His face clenched on what looked like suffering as he raised himself on his arms. "Stop...I'm hurting you..."

She clung harder. "Only at first—now—*ya Ullah ya* Rashid—the pleasure of you inside me—I never knew anything could feel like this—that I could ever feel so much pleasure. But I need more, everything, as you promised me. Give it all to me, Rashid...*arjook*..."

"Anti sehr, j'noon..." His growl, declaring her magic and madness, was that of a man at the end of his tether. It zapped through her with its ferociousness, its desperation, with the hope he would finally give in, give her everything.

And he did. He drove back all the way to the recesses of her essence. Then, holding her gaze, his own as feverish as she knew hers must be, he began to move.

Each glide layered pleasure upon pleasure, burying her

under an avalanche. With each stretching of her slick tissues around his invasion, she fell further apart, her surrender to *his* magic and madness deepening. Needing even more, her demands for it rose until his gentleness caught the fire of urgency, then ferocity, until everything was condensed into one pinpoint of absolute existence where he was plunging deepest inside her. Then it exploded.

She came apart, unraveling on shrieks of his name. She shattered then reformed around his thickness with every discharge, her core straining to drain all the pleasure he was driving into her body. He roared her name, stiffened in her arms, plunged deeper, breaching her completely as jets of his seed filled her. She writhed and wept from the sheer pleasure inundating her, with feeling his release surge against her intimate flesh, his weight and feel as he anchored her in the storm completion itself.

With her body replete to its last cell, lips open on labored breaths and his scar, the world spiraled down into a dark, safe place of contentment—the depths of his embrace….

In a dream state of pervasive bliss, sensations coalesced. She was lying on top of something hot and hard but so perfectly comfortable. And emanating steady, restrained booms.

A roughened caress swept down her back to cup her buttock. No dream had ever felt so bone-meltingly good, so mind-messingly arousing. She opened her eyes, met his.

Rashid. The best thing she'd ever woken up to.

Lying beneath her like a sleek black panther, it was evident he'd been long awake. And watching her.

Delight blossomed at the sight of him, spreading her lips, weighing down her lids, melting everything else. "I'd say good morning, but it would be the understatement of the millennium."

His caresses continued, igniting every inch they smoothed. "A new adjective has to be coined to describe it, yes."

Joy quivered in her heart. He thought the same in the cold light of day. He didn't regret it.

But that look in his eyes…it was new. Nothing she understood…

"I have an adjective for last night, though. Life-changing."

On that, too, they agreed. Though she was surprised he thought so. He wasn't the one who'd been saved by the person he'd loved all his life then ended up begging her to take his virginity, which she did while teaching him what ecstasy was.

But she wasn't about to look that gift miracle in the mouth.

She stretched languorously over his great body, delighting that he was big enough to sleep on, that he seemed to derive as much pleasure from being slept on.

Her voice came out a purr when she said, "And then some."

"*Aih.* Neither of our lives will ever be the same again now that they will be forever entwined."

She raised her head, stared at him. The way he'd said *that.* And that intent look. He couldn't possibly mean…

In the next moment, he ended speculation. "Through marriage."

Seven

"Marriage!"

Laylah's incredulity echoed in the huge room as she scrambled up from Rashid's embrace.

She gaped at him as he, too, rose to a sitting position, totally uncaring of his nakedness, or the fact that he was still gloriously aroused. Or maybe he always woke up in the morning like that…?

Focus, moron. Not the time to be drooling over his assets or reliving what he'd done to her with them when he'd just said…said…

"Marriage!"

The word rang out again before she could hold it back.

But who could blame her? Yesterday, she'd woken up never expecting to see Rashid again. Today she woke up in his bed, and he was already talking…

No! She *wasn't* going to squeak it out again.

His hand reached out to smooth a long tress off her hot, damp cheek. "Of course. I took your innocence and I don't—"

"Don't." His words hit her like a bucket of ice water in the face. Embarrassed at her nakedness all of a sudden, she groped for the covers she'd kicked to the bottom of the mattress a lifetime ago. "Just don't even start on *that*."

Having Rashid in her life at all was a miracle. Having Rashid as her husband was beyond imaginable. But she was damned if she'd let this progress to a bona fide offer based on *that* reason.

"You didn't 'take my innocence', I *gave* it to you. And will you stop being so archaic and so—so…Azmaharian? Innocence, indeed. So now I'm, what, because you've 'taken' it—wicked?"

The eyes that had hardened and cooled with her every word suddenly softened, heated. "Indeed. But then, you were already that as an innocent. Now the mind boggles at what levels of devastation you'll attain in your…newly forged wickedness."

Heat splashed through her as she remembered in detail how *he'd*…forged said wickedness inside her…

Catching her swollen-from-his-passion-and-stinging-for-more lip in her teeth and letting the cover go, she leaned to rub her face against his chest. "Why don't we find out?"

He caught her by the shoulders as her lips strayed over his flesh, held her off, his smile filling with indulgence. "We will. We have a lifetime to make extensive explorations of every iota of your potential for sensual mayhem."

There he went again, talking about lifetimes. Nothing she wanted more than to have several of those entwined with him, but *not* if it was prodded by his outdated sense of honor.

She pulled back, this time wrapping the cover around her. "Listen, Rashid, I already told you in embarrassing detail how I had this hopeless passion for you. It turns out I didn't have a clue what passion was all about, something you've rectified with enough clues to fill this place. If I thought I wanted you before, now I *know,* and just how fiercely and totally. If you want me with anything approaching that ferocity and totality, then there's nothing more that I want than to be with you. Just not 'through marriage.'"

And she realized the real meaning of yet another word. *Ominous*. That had to be what defined that scowl.

"You're refusing to marry me?"

Her heartstrings shook at the darkness in his rumble. "I'm refusing to introduce the concept of 'marriage' at this point."

And if displeasure could take form, it would wear just that face, and lash out with that solar-flare-level glare. "Marriage between us now is not a concept, it's a necessity."

"Oh, please, not the 'innocence' thing again. I wasn't saving it for an eventual groom and you did not come and 'take advantage' of my 'vulnerability' and now you don't have to offer yourself at the altar of honor and propriety!"

"You *were* saving it. If you don't subscribe to our region's values, why else are you—*were* you—still a virgin at this age?"

"*Gah*…at *this* age? *Et tu,* Brute?"

"Laylah!"

His warning growl was the essence of deliciousness. She grinned into his stern eyes. "I do subscribe to some regional values, but certainly not this one. So I'll refer you to my previous confession for the answer to this question and every other you have now or might have in the future."

"What confession?"

"Do you forget it every time I say it? That I wanted *you* all my life, of course. What other confession did I make?"

"I remember a night-long medley of revelations."

She nudged him playfully in the ribs. "Admit it, I'm entertaining." A twitch almost undid his lips' disapproving rigidity. Her grin widened. "As for finding me in mint condition at this advanced age, it's only because I wasn't about to jump in bed with anyone else when all I wanted was you. You could say I was pointlessly saving it for you. So when fate provided both you and a bed, well—you have firsthand experience with how things progressed. Terminally chivalrous, you did your level best to ward me off, to make me back down. But I left you nowhere to run."

"I've beaten back armies, pulverized my way out of sieges

in war zones—on front lines, in boardrooms and in the market. The only reason I didn't 'ward you off' was because I didn't want to. Because I wanted you so much, I didn't even stop when I found out you were—yes, here it comes again—an innocent."

Her heart tap-danced at the momentous confession. That she'd been the one thing Rashid hadn't been able to resist, and his desire for her the one thing he hadn't been able to conquer.

Her grin grew teasing, even as her eyes filled with joy. "Take heart. By the time you found out, I was no longer any such thing. But how can you compare me to armies and adversaries? Their attacks only made you stronger, made beating them that much easier. Against my desire, you didn't have a prayer."

His grimness deepened as he exhaled. "You got that right. I was never exposed to anything like you. I didn't know anything like you existed. You…overpower me."

She fell back on her heels, rocked to her core. That confession was more than huge. It was historic.

But the way he'd said it… "You—you resent that?"

His focus sharpened on her. *"No."* The force of his denial defused her rising anxiety. "But…it's something I have no experience with. I could never abide accepting anything from anyone. Then you come along…" His hand traveled up her arm to her neck then her check, cupping it. "The way you want me, what you give me and how much I want it and you—it's so unknown, I have no idea how to handle it."

"You've handled it all flawlessly so far." She threw herself at him, hugged him with all her strength. "But if you feel as shaken to your core as I do, are no longer sure if you're coming or going like I am, that's all the more reason to take it slowly and not jump into something as big as marriage." She raised her face to his. "How about we take it one day at a time? And after a reasonable time—let's say a month, if you can still stand me—you can bring up marriage again?" She pinched his hard cheek. "And if that comes to pass, I'd appreciate an offer, not a decree."

He arched an eyebrow adamantly. "I won't wait a month.

Not even a day, if it means I won't have you in my bed in the interim."

"Bed? What bed?" She chuckled at the lion's rumble that reverberated in his gut and melted back against him, indulgence turning her to goo. "Down boy. I wouldn't dream of staying out of your...mattress. In fact, after last night, you just try to keep me off it. And if it was as incredible for you as it was for me..."

Those scrumptiously serious eyes became solemn. "I might not have been an innocent, but what I experienced with you *was* a first. I meant it when I said last night was life-changing."

Delight gripped her heart so fiercely she feared it might pierce it. "Then it would be downright self-destructive if we didn't indulge in this activity as frequently as humanly possible. But there are many more areas where we need to see if we're *that* compatible."

"Last night proved we are, in all areas that matter. You were right when you said we are not strangers. That has to be why we connected so smoothly and deeply."

She laughed. "Sure. Connecting my tentacles deeply into you sure went smoothly. You've set a new record for Male Struggles Against Female Advances."

"My struggles were a misguided attempt at chivalry, as you so correctly diagnosed." His eyes lost that gravity, grew heated, hungered. "No more struggling, ever again."

"That's better news than anything I ever dared hope for. So can't you let me, let us, savor this?" She smoothed out his gathering frown. "What's the rush?"

She caught a relenting glimmer in his eyes, something she was starting to realize meant he was softening inside. "The rush is that your power, which your mother and aunt clearly knew nothing about, is so overwhelming, you shredded my ironclad control. I took you without protection. You might already be pregnant."

The wish for that to be true was so intense, she couldn't breathe.

When she could draw air again she said, "That's still not a

reason to rush into marriage." Even if it was the struggle of her life not to jump on his offer. "I have to admit *you* were right. We don't know a lot about each other."

"We know enough. All the important things."

Feeling herself on the verge of giving in, she tried again. "Why not take the time to know all the unimportant things, too? I hear those are usually what make people turn each others' lives into hell and end up breaking them apart." She ran a teasing finger down the cleft in his chin. "Maybe in a month's time I'll find you an incredible bore and you'll find me an unbearable pain in the neck, and we'll both be glad we didn't rush into anything."

His arm tugged her closer, pulling her into his rock-hard body. "Wanting like this would counteract any boredom you might feel. And it would relieve any neck pain I might suffer." Before she could argue more, he had her spread and open beneath him. "But though I believe we don't need it, you can have your month. As long as I have you all through it. And it's not one day longer."

Then he took her lips, took her. She welcomed him back into her body, her heart soaring.

She only hoped that by month's end, his insistence on legitimizing their passion would no longer be driven by any hint of honor, commitment and duty. She wanted the passion itself to be the only reason.

Though what she really yearned for was that he would come to love her. As much as she loved him.

One miracle at a time, she reminded herself, as she drowned in his passion and pleasure again.

"Can we have a bed?"

Laylah stretched her arms up in the air, savoring the soreness in her every muscle as she walked back to Rashid. He was awaiting her return on that mattress where he'd been taking her to heavens she hadn't known existed for the past week.

"Not that I don't love that mattress. Literally the best time of my life has been spent on it. I just want some…variation."

He caught her hand, brought her down on his lap, ensconcing her within his great body. "We can have anything at all that you want. If I don't anticipate your wishes, just ask."

Which would be impossible to do. Since their first night together, he'd not only been anticipating her wishes but doing things for her she hadn't even known to wish for. Like taking her on a surprise flight on his private jet to visit Mira in Tennessee. And surprising her with an ingenious analysis report that would see her business jumping to a whole new level.

He seemed to be thinking of her every minute of the day, and what he could do for her. In his own unique way, he was doing something she'd never dreamed he'd do. He was courting her.

As if she needed to love him more. But she did as he wooed and watched over her, as he pleasured and possessed her. With every word and touch and action, he kept dragging her deeper in love with him. Every moment she shared with him, every breath and glance, was every dream she hadn't dared believe would come true.

And he hadn't kept her just to his personal time and domain. He'd shown her his business side, letting her see how a master negotiated deals and waged war, teaching her tricks she couldn't wait to implement in her own business, tutoring her in the methods of maximum efficiency with minimum effort and time. He let her in on his every secret method, thought process and strategy. He was intense about everything, brilliant in every way.

But what surprised her most was how sensitive and caring he was, in his own subtle, practical, effective way. Not only with her, in and out of bed, but with his people. His right-hand man, Ahmad, had told her yesterday that Rashid's army of deputies and underlings worshipped the dirt under his feet, would walk into an inferno for him. She believed it.

It was a validation of how right she'd been about him all her life. He was everything she'd ever admired and respected. He was her hero in every way.

She couldn't imagine how anyone could contemplate anyone else for the throne of Azmahar. In her opinion, no king in history had ever been more qualified.

"I just want a bed," she said, coming up for breath from his last kiss.

Passion blazed in his black eyes, but his voice betrayed some lightness. "I just gave you carte blanche. Do it justice, *ya ameerati,* use it well."

"I did tell you I'm no good at asking for or accepting stuff. I'm no good at *wanting* stuff. I really want nothing else. So... I'll just keep this carte blanche to use well in...other areas."

"In *those* areas, you already have carte rainbow. But in *this* area, I'm ahead of you. I've already ordered everything that will turn this place into the sensual wonderland where I can do your voluptuous magnificence justice, with all the props that will give me every...variation to pleasure and service you into oblivion."

If he was already redecorating his place for her, this had to be serious, and long-term. Oh, sure, he'd already asked her to marry him. But that had been driven by honor as much as passion.

This was all passion.

Overwhelmed with joy, she whispered, "I want one more thing."

"Name it."

She ran hands trembling with longing to and fro over his head, the dense, cropped silk covering it feeling like velvet beneath her aching palms. "Grow your hair back."

His caresses stilled, his expression shuttering closed.

Had she tripped one of his proximity sensors? Did he find it easy to give her material things, let her come as close as could be sexually, but when it came to emotional intimacy, he balked?

Just as she was kicking herself for presuming too much, too

soon, he pulled her closer, flattening her breasts against his chest, his eyes searing into her soul.

Then he said, "Done."

Forgetting her decision to never again make such demands of him, she whooped, jumped in his arms, deluged him in kisses before pulling back, letting her greed take over. "Mid-back? In a ponytail?"

His lips twisted. "How about we take it an inch at a time?"

"That's payback for my 'day at a time,' isn't it?"

He wouldn't admit to it, but she knew. He wasn't thrilled about waiting. But it thrilled her that he wasn't badgering her into an early acceptance. That he was letting them experience this phase of their relationship, enjoy its wonders.

He rose, swinging her up in his arms, making her feel weightless. "Let's explore some of the new props."

"You mean you already have some here?"

"You mean you didn't notice the new additions? I thought they'd stick out in the void downstairs."

"With you meeting me at the door and taking me against it, before hauling me here semiconscious with pleasure? I wouldn't have noticed if said void had been engulfed in a meteor crater."

"Now that might not be a bad idea. A crater I'd fill with perfect temperature water." Somehow holding her with one arm as he descended the stairs, he smoothed his knuckles against her cheek tenderly. "Would you like an indoor swimming pool?"

Afraid she'd pour through his arms, she sighed. "A huge tub with you in it? Well, duh!"

He sat her down on what she realized was a swing.

As her imagination flooded with erotic possibilities for *that* "prop," he gave her lower lip an approving nip. "Duh it is, then."

"So why is Laylah not staying with you?"

Mira's question caused Laylah to look at Rashid intently as he drove all three of them back from an excellent dinner out.

For the past three weeks he'd been sharing something new with her every day. Picnics, hikes, business trips, museums, shows. Intimate rendezvouses at his place and then at secluded hideaways while the pool had been installed. Tonight he'd taken her—and Mira—to an incredible restaurant for another unprecedented experience.

"I mean," Mira went on from the backseat, her voice half an octave higher as always in Rashid's presence. "You return her so late every night it's always after I go to sleep."

Rashid looked at Mira in the mirror with that tranquility that Laylah knew indicated unending patience with her for being *her* best friend. It still amazed her that there wasn't the least bit of male appreciation in his eyes for the fiery and statuesque beauty who turned heads wherever they went.

He inclined his head in gallant apology. "I am sorry if I've been the reason for disturbing your sleep."

"That's not what I meant!" Mira spluttered, as always out of her depth around Rashid.

Laylah could sympathize big-time. Rashid's larger-than-life vibe could mess with anyone's balance. Especially those with XX chromosomes. It had to be loving him that much, and his unlimited indulgence with her, that made her function somewhat normally around him.

Mira elaborated, "Hey, I've been having the time of my life with you guys these past weeks. I love the ride home every day from work in this wonder car, and in the company of my favorite couple in the world. And I can't tell you how much I appreciate all that wish-fulfillment stuff you keep pulling—flying me in private jets, getting round-the-clock medical attention for Dad at home and taking me out with you to places I didn't know existed, not to mention the magic wand you've touched our business with. I'm just wondering, since you've been condensing your working hours to the bare minimum to make more time for each other, why not stay in the same place to have even more time together?"

"According to Laylah," Rashid said, "it's because I'm terminally archaic and can't evolve beyond my Azmaharian programming."

Yeah. She'd told him that. And a few more elaborate frustrations. He would be with her only during "appropriate" hours. But he wouldn't hear of her spending the nights at his place, or her reputation would evidently disintegrate to ashes. The only time she'd spent the night with him had been that first night.

But that paled in comparison to another matter.

Tonight was their one-month anniversary.

At least it had been. Now after midnight, the day had passed.

And Rashid hadn't asked her to marry him again.

She'd remained on pins and needles all day, thinking he'd say something during their late lunch. He hadn't. Then at dinner, he'd invited Mira along and had so far said nothing.

Because Mira was around? Why invite her if she'd cramp his style? What did it all mean?

Had he rethought his offer? Decided it had been rushed and rash? With her being so free with her favors, maybe he thought he'd been wrong to worry about her "honor" when she wasn't worried about it herself. Maybe he thought he should just enjoy what they had.

She'd want that, too, as long as it was long-term. But what if his change of heart meant that whatever he thought they had wouldn't last long? What if he started winding down gradually to an inevitable end? Maybe he'd made that decision early on, and that was why he'd been adamant about her not moving in or even staying the occasional night. Maybe he didn't want to cloak their intimacies in any kind of permanence.

She tried to shake off her doubts, listen to the almost one-sided conversation between Mira and Rashid. She couldn't.

He pulled up to their building and said good-night to Mira, who responded with the self-possession of a starstruck schoolgirl, before she exited the car, murmuring for Laylah to take her time.

She didn't. After a kiss that she initiated and he ended too soon, Rashid said that he had to rush away.

She stood on the sidewalk watching him drive off, feeling a chill that had nothing to do with the weather creeping into her bones. She hadn't thought twice about what it meant any other night when he'd dropped her at her place and driven off. But tonight…

Could it be he didn't realize what tonight was?

No. No way. Rashid forgot nothing. And since he'd said nothing, maybe he just had nothing to say.

It was a long time after he'd disappeared that she'd dejectedly turned and entered the building.

Unable to face Mira again, she waited outside their apartment, struggling with tears, until she heard silence inside.

Once in her room, she rushed into the shower, dissolved the hot tears she could no longer hold back in hotter water, as suspicions overtook her thoughts.

Why had he insisted on Mira's presence tonight of all nights? Had he needed her as a buffer against any possibility of intimacy? Today *had* been the first day without any form of that. Had he considered today, instead of being the beginning of a new phase in their relationship, to be the beginning of the end? Had her prophecy come to pass? A month in her company had been more than enough, and she'd started to grate on him?

But last night he'd made love to her with as much hunger as ever. Was that not enough anymore, and being the chivalrous knight that he was, he was trying to find a painless way out of this mess? What would she do if this was true?

After a night in a hell of uncertainty, morning brought with it the searing light of realization. Why Rashid was pulling away.

It had to be because she'd told him she loved him.

At first, it had been in the throes of passion, then gradually afterward she'd said it at every opportunity. She hadn't worried when he hadn't said it back. She'd thought it had been too soon for him, but she had been certain it was coming.

What if, instead of being truthful with him about her emotions, as she'd thought she should be, she'd only pressured him? And his response to her fervor, when he believed he couldn't reciprocate it, was to pull away?

Unable to hold back anymore, anxiety and urgency eating

through her restraint, she snatched her phone up, dialed his number.

He picked up on the second ring. She recognized the background sounds. He was in his car.

"Laylah—"

She cut him off before he could say anything more. "I didn't…didn't mean anything when I said I loved you. Please, just forget I said it."

Eight

A cacophony of sounds was all Rashid heard after Laylah told him to forget she'd told him she loved him.

It wasn't until a policeman knocked on his window that Rashid realized the noise was a storm of honking.

He'd braked in the middle of the street.

He didn't remember ending the call with her, or what exactly he said to the policeman. He only knew he found himself parked in front of the entrance of her building, staring up at her window, one thing pummeling through him.

She'd come to her senses.

He'd been dreading she would. Almost waiting for her to.

He shouldn't have waited. He should have pushed for marriage sooner. But he'd been terrified he'd scare her away, yet it had been hell trying to pull back. But it had also been a heaven he hadn't known existed, being with her. Being loved by her.

For she *had* loved him. Her love had been so pure and intense, had permeated him from her every touch and word and action, he'd basked in its unbelievable blessing with every breath. He hadn't known how or why she'd loved him, but she *had*.

He'd been trying to tell himself that, with Laylah being so overt about her emotions, when she agreed to marry him, no one would suspect that their marriage was not for the right reasons. That it would serve his purpose, get him everything he'd planned.

But with every hour in her company, every other consideration had ceased to exist. Nothing mattered anymore but her. Everything from her, with her, had overwhelmed him, undone him. With her he'd finally understood what happiness was.

But he'd left it too late. Even when he'd done everything in his power to stop her from realizing the truth about him, time had exposed him to her for what he was. A damaged, dangerous monster.

What had he expected? He shouldn't have been in her heart in the first place. He didn't deserve to be there.

Without knowing how, he found himself on her apartment doorstep just as she opened her door.

A huge gasp escaped her at the sight of him, the streams of tears already pouring down her face thickening.

Feeling sorry for him? Regretting that she had to let him down?

He couldn't bear for her to feel bad. Never on his account. He'd sacrifice anything for her to never shed another tear.

Before he could say anything, she dragged him inside, her eyes all over him before she hugged him with all her strength, smothering her face in his chest.

"Rashid, *ya Ullah,* Rashid…you're okay, you're okay…"

Struck to his core at feeling her against him again, he stood, unable to move in her embrace, everything inside him demolished.

"I went insane when I heard that commotion and the line went dead and I couldn't call you back. I thought you had an accident…"

Her voice broke on a sob that fractured his muteness, made him choke, "I'm sorry I scared you."

"What matters is that you're okay." Suddenly, she undid her frantic hold on him, embarrassment in her every line as she moved away. "I—I meant what I said, Rashid."

That she wanted him to forget that she'd said she loved him.

He owed her the complete truth, if only in this. "How can I ever forget the one real honor and profound joy I ever had? The memory that you once loved me will fuel the rest of my life, and at its end, will be my one worthwhile achievement."

Confusion then stupefaction gripped her loveliness.

Then she blurted out, "What do you mean 'once'? You think I...? Oh, no, Rashid, I only meant I wasn't pushing you to reciprocate when I said I love you. I had no other purpose behind it but telling you how I feel. I thought you felt pressured by my confessions because the month I asked for is up and you didn't—didn't..."

It was his turn to be flabbergasted.

"You thought..." He stopped, hope too joyous, too brutal. "You thought your declarations of love made me *reconsider my proposal?*"

Delightful peach invaded her honeyed cheeks. "I didn't know what to think, so I thought the worst. Y-you must know what yesterday was."

"It was the one-month anniversary of the attack. But this morning, this *hour,* is the one-month anniversary of my proposal."

Her eyes rounded on still-fragile hope. "Y-you mean...?"

"I mean I was coming at the exact time I proposed last month, this time to ask...to *beg* that you consider marriage. Not because I want you and because my honor dictates it. But because my life would mean nothing anymore without you."

Suddenly, his arms were full of hurtling, clinging love and eagerness made flesh and blood. And he wrapped himself around her, containing her, vowing to never let her go again.

Those minutes when he'd thought he'd lost her had hurt far more than the injury that had left him scarred, had been more desperate than any time he'd thought he'd die.

Deluging him in kisses, Laylah buried her fingers in the hair he was growing back for her, her voice a throb of silk and night and hunger. "My life would mean nothing without you, too. It never did. I love you with everything I am, Rashid…"

Reeling with disbelief that this perfect being continued to love him, he carried her where he could seal the magic of those moments with that of their passion and turn the once-impossible fantasy into reality.

What felt like a lifetime later, but what was actually only a couple of hours, still overcome with Rashid's last possession and the echoes of the aborted scare, Laylah stretched luxuriously against his hot, hard body.

His beloved face was flushed a marvelous copper tone. His whisper, when it came, spread its dark compulsion inside her. "Do I take it all that was a yes?"

She snuggled into his body more securely. "You mean you didn't hear any of the hundreds of yeses I said? I must have raised Chicago's noise pollution levels to an all-time high."

"Just give me one now that your blood has cooled."

She rubbed her thigh against his. "You mean you don't know yet that you and cool blood are mutually exclusive?"

His arms gathered her into his body with such tender reverence, trembling with the same emotion that blazed in his eyes. "Laylah…give it to me. One yes. Total and final."

And she gave it to him. Her irrevocable pledge. "Yes, Rashid. As total as my whole being and final to my life's end."

His groan was one of relief and elation as he took her lips, sealing their lifelong pact.

As she surrendered her all to him yet again, it felt different this time. She'd always been his, but this time, in her very essence, she became his wife.

* * *

Before Mira returned from work, Rashid took Laylah back to his place. It was evening when he took a break from branding her with his most tender lovemaking ever, carried her to the shower, then to the kitchen, where they now delighted in cooking together.

He was handing her the pesto he'd prepared to add to the pasta she had made when she said, "Do you have a preference for how exactly we should get married? Mc, I'd like a tiny ceremony."

His hand froze midway with the pesto. Then he placed it on the island, pulled her to him. "We can't start thinking of the ceremony yet. Accepting me is only half the battle won."

She squinted up at him, perplexed. "What do you mean *half?*"

"Now I need to go win the other half. Your family."

"What do *they* have to do with anything between us? The most involvement they'll have is to get stuffed in their fineries and come to our wedding. Those I'll *let* attend. *If* they behave." His hands cupped her face. For the first time ever, she removed them. "You're not talking me out of this, Rashid. My family stays out of our lives, and that's final."

His eyes grew watchful, as if he was gauging how to handle her sudden volatility. "If it were up to me, I would have vowed myself to you in absolute seclusion. But you are a princess…"

"Oh, no. You're *not* princessing me again!"

He coaxed her into his arms again, caressing resistance out of her a nerve at a time. "I know you want it not to matter, but it does. Tradition is important, even when it's infuriating. But this won't only be about us. It will be about our children." The concept of children, his and hers, liquefied something inside her. "I want there to be peace and acceptance surrounding our union from the start, for you, for them. What makes things a bit more complicated is that I'm not a prince…"

"You're worth a thousand of every prince who ever lived!"

Pride and pleasure glittered in his eyes, softened his lips. "Your approval and allegiance mean *everything.* To me. But I need to get theirs, too. Your family includes some very powerful individuals, and I'm not on their right side to start with. I don't want them to bother you with their disapproval or attempts to come between us. I need to…defuse their danger."

"And how are you supposed to do that?"

"As per tradition, your family tribunal will make demands of me and put me through trials, as outrageous as they can make them. They'll agree to give me your hand in marriage only once I pass all their tests and meet all their requirements."

"Shades of Antarah ibn Shaddad when Ablah's father asked for a thousand red camels to stymie him! I'm all for defusing their danger, but I draw the line at hurtling back in time to the eleventh century to do it."

"That's what tradition is—age-old practices."

"I have nothing against those when they're about innocuous stuff like food or design or celebrations. But I'm damned if I bow to traditions that delete centuries of progress and make me some prize to be won for the right price. I might as well throw away my master's degrees in business management and information technology. How would I be different from any tent-bound maiden bartered to whomever haggled with her elders for her, before carrying her away as one of his possessions, a bit above his goat, but certainly beneath his horse and sword?"

"In my case, it would be private jets and multinational corporations." She rewarded his teasing with a rib nudge. His eyes softened as he gathered her more securely against his hard body. "We'll just play along to save headaches."

"You really intend to submit to such a…*ridiculous* practice?"

"I will, *ya habibati.* Like I will worship you with my body and serve and protect you with my wealth and strength, I will submit to anything to honor you before your family and the world. I want there to be no doubt to what lengths I would go to, to have the privilege of your choice, the power of your love."

And what could she say to *that?*

Resistance almost gone, she tried one last thing. "But according to this moronic tradition, if ten percent of *awleya'a el amr*—the elders—refuse you, you won't be able to marry me."

Something inexorable came into his eyes. "I will have zero percent refusals. Failure is not an option."

Nine

For years, Rashid had considered returning to Zohayd an impossibility. Now he wasn't just back in the country, he was in a limo heading to Zohayd's royal palace, a place he'd sworn never to tread again.

But then he was sitting right next to another impossibility. Laylah. Who loved him. Who wanted him. Who believed in him.

Having her by his side made returning to Zohayd...bearable.

This was the land where he'd spent too many years watching Laylah from afar, unable to return her glances or reciprocate her interest. Where he'd found and lost those he'd thought of as brothers given to him by fate in exchange for taking everyone else away from him. Where he'd suffered the betrayal that had left him mutilated.

Then, claiming the kingship of Azmahar had become his life's goal, and he'd known he'd be forced to return to Zohayd one day. But even when he'd started his plan, he hadn't imagined this would be how he'd return. With Laylah as his world, not his pawn.

The supple hand entwined with his tugged him out of the darkness of his memories and worries to the sunniness of her smile and reality. "So who's waiting for us at the palace?"

"I informed King Atef. I assume he'll tell everyone else."

Her grin widened. "Word of advice. Don't use the word *king* around Uncle Atef. He hurled the title at Amjad and seems to want to forget the decades when he was one."

"He's been King Atef to me since I can remember. It'll be very difficult to think of him as plain Sheikh Atef now. And of Amjad as king."

"I know what you mean. Amjad is such a virtuoso in infuriating everyone and pulverizing rules and protocols, I thought he'd bring Zohayd down in a week when he became king. But though he's taken being outrageous to a new realm, he's now head-to-head with Aliyah's Kamal for the position of best king in the region's history." She snuggled deeper into him, her smile catching the fire of adoration that he now felt he needed to sustain his vital functions. "Of course, the region hasn't seen *you* as king yet."

His heart trembled at how he'd come to depend on her esteem and belief. At how he felt he didn't deserve them. "You always talk as if becoming a king is a sure thing for me."

"I can't see how it isn't. You're the absolute best man for the role, ever. Apart from my opinion, you're a pureblooded Azmaharian, a decorated war hero and your success in business has surpassed even Haidar's and Jalal's. *And* you're an Aal Munsoori."

"Azmaharians hate that name now."

Her expression became adorably serious. "They hate only one branch of the family, but still think of the Aal Munsooris at large as their rightful monarchs." Her smile dawned again as her eyes devoured him. "And if anyone ever looked the part, it's you." Her hands strayed all over his shoulders and chest… and lower. "They must have coined the adjective *regal* for you."

He caught her hands, his gaze shooting to the partition between the limo's compartments. Even though he knew Ahmad couldn't see or hear them, he didn't want to start something he might not be able to stop. And he'd made a decision that, while in their region, he wouldn't do anything to compromise her image.

It was still almost beyond his ability to deprive them both of the needed pleasure. He was almost panting when he said, "You're clearly not in the least biased."

She lay back against him, her hands captured in his, her eyes gobbling him up. "I am the essence of impartiality. If Azmaharians know what's best for them, they'll choose you."

"If they do, how do you feel about becoming their queen?"

Her blink was surprise itself.

Would *she* ever stop surprising him? "You didn't think of it?"

She sat up, her smooth forehead furrowing. "Uh…thinking wasn't among my priorities this past month. But then I not only didn't connect the dots between you becoming king and me becoming queen, I never contemplated being one, when it was all my mother thought of making me, too."

His heart contracted at what *he* hadn't contemplated. "It would be an unwelcome burden? A life you wouldn't want for yourself or our children?"

The eyes that always shone with appreciation and humor grew somber. "It *would* be a huge responsibility and a radical change. It would take as drastic an adjustment." Before he could blurt out that he would never disrupt her peace, that he would forget his kingship ambitions, her eyes glowed with conviction. "But I'll share your choices and your life's developments no matter what they are. If it's your destiny to become king, then it's my destiny to become your queen."

And he forgot his abstinence resolution. His arms convulsed around her, his lips mashing to her forehead, to her cheeks, her lips, his heart overflowing. *"Habibati…"*

A rap on the limo's window jerked him out of his surrender to poignancy. It had Laylah starting out of his embrace, too.

They both turned to find Amjad Aal Shalaan, Laylah's oldest cousin and the infernal king of Zohayd, smirking down at them through the window.

Rashid hadn't realized they'd been nearing the palace let alone that they were already there.

Shielding her from Amjad's eyes, giving her time to rearrange anything he'd mussed, he opened the door and glared up at the man whose alliance he was supposed to court.

Even before Amjad's transformation into a manipulative, borderline insane son of a bitch after his first wife had nearly poisoned him to death, he'd always rubbed Rashid the wrong way. There'd always been something about Amjad that reminded him too much of himself.

Against all expectations, Amjad had married again. Maram Aal Waaked, the daughter of the ruling prince of a neighboring emirate, Ossaylan. Amjad had tried to use Maram to force her father to return the Pride of Zohayd jewels, which, according to Zohaydan law and legend, conferred the right to rule the kingdom. It had turned out Maram's hapless father had been blackmailed by the ex-queen of Zohayd, Sondoss, Laylah's aunt, into helping her steal the jewels. Reportedly, Amjad had fallen flat on his face in love with Maram. Now after he'd been dubbed the Mad Prince, he'd become the Crazy King—crazy in love with his new wife.

That Rashid had to see to believe.

All he saw now was Amjad's provocation as he met those startlingly emerald eyes on the same level. Not that he needed more than Amjad's rude interruption of his tender moment with Laylah to guarantee his hackles wouldn't subside for the foreseeable future.

"King Amjad," he gritted between clenched teeth in lieu of a punch in the nose.

"Sheikh Rashid." Devilry danced in Amjad's eyes as he inclined his head. "Rumor has it you're here on a bid to cure my cousin's chronic spinsterhood."

Before he could respond to that insolence, Laylah squeezed his arm, no doubt to stop him from putting his fist through her cousin's and king's smirking face. He'd been insane if he thought he could ally himself with this incorrigible creature.

"It's so good to see being a harassed king and a henpecked husband hasn't defanged you, Amjad," Laylah said merrily.

Amjad continued talking about her as if she wasn't there. "But then she's been trying to catch your eye since she could toddle. Oh, yes, we all noticed. And cringed. It was excruciating watching her pant after you. Made me hyperventilate. So how did she suddenly succeed in curing *your* blindness to her splendor?"

The wily wolf was skeptical. Rashid had known he would be. Amjad had suspicion for blood. It was why he'd originally hatched this whole plan. To pass Amjad's maximum-distrust inspection.

Amjad continued, "It *was* weird, how determined you were in not noticing her. It got so fishy, I asked Haidar and Jalal if they knew which team you played for."

Against his better judgment, Rashid said, "There were years when speculation about *your* team loyalties ran rampant, too."

Amjad's grin grew more goading, delighted that he'd gotten a rise from him. "*I* didn't have a smitten angel hero-worshipping me for years."

"I hear Queen Maram did just that before you rethought your…predilections."

Amjad's eyes blazed greener. The bastard loved this. "Those were only put on hold after my monster bride slathered me in arsenic. That's a good enough reason to swear off women for a few years, don't you think? What was your excuse?"

It was no use. This would develop into a full-scale war.

So be it. And to hell with his alliance. "While you were getting over your self-pitying and preserving neurosis, I was serving my country and putting my life on the line for the region's safety. I didn't think it fair to involve a woman in a life that could end prematurely."

Laylah's convulsive dig into his arm transmitted how horrifying she found the what-if scenario.

He squeezed her hand, warding off the imaginary dread, re-assuring her that he was here, would always be here, with her.

Amjad, not missing a thing, continued his inflammatory interrogation. "But that heroic existence came to an end a few years ago. What reminded you of my worshipping cousin all of a sudden? And made you not only look her way this time, but decide to take her off the shelf, and in record time, too?"

He decided to tell both of them the truth about this at least. "The reason I never looked at you—" he turned his eyes to Laylah, whose eyes filled with tears and wonder as she heard his confession for the first time "—wasn't because I didn't no-tice you, or wasn't interested. I was, painfully so. But I wasn't worthy of looking in your direction then."

Amjad let out a deriding guffaw. "And you think you are now?"

Laylah stepped between them. "Are you two gigantic boys done chest-thumping, or do you need to release some more tes-tosterone? Why don't you just beat each other black and blue and get this 'who's the bigger, badder alpha' thing out of your systems?"

Rashid watched as Amjad looked down with extreme amuse-ment at Laylah, who cared not a bit that he was one of the most powerful men in the world, smacking him in chastisement, as if he was only her exasperating—and younger—relative and not her king.

Jealousy radiated up Rashid's spine. Cousin or not, he wanted her to smack no other male, wanted no other male to revel in being smacked by her.

Amjad gave her a mock bow. "For knock-down, drag-out fights, and any other physically expressed stupidity, I'll refer you to Harres. Or Jalal. Me, my wit is my lash, my tongue my sword."

Fighting the need to shove him away from Laylah, Rashid said, "You imagine you wield such weapons, when it's your status that stops people from showing you their real worth in a fair fight."

Amjad pretended shock. "You mean you're holding back in respect for my status?" He wiggled his eyebrows at him. "I hereby decree you're free to do your best. Or is it only your worst?"

Again Laylah came between them, this time one palm flat on each of their chests, keeping them apart. "Down boys. In your corners."

Amjad sighed. "Okay. Just because Rashid is an endangered species and we need him alive and able to breed. I don't think we'd find you another mate if he expires."

Laylah dug her elbow in Amjad's gut, her smile so radiant as she looked up, asking Rashid to share the joke. He only wanted to poke Amjad's green eyes out.

Turning to Amjad, she asked, "Is my father here?"

"You expected him to be?" Amjad scoffed. "That deadbeat? And I thought you were above such sentimental tripe. If you haven't yet, it's time to face it already, Laylah. In *that* generation only one apple didn't turn out rotten. *My* father is all we got in the way of a parent around this place."

An incensed step brought Rashid slamming into Amjad chest-first. "Even if she knows the truth about her father, it doesn't mean it doesn't still hurt her. You don't have to be cruel."

"Oh, I assure you, I have to." Amjad's eyes suddenly smoldered with something besides mockery. Fury. "It's called tough love, and she's better off considering *both* her parents as dead as my mother or your parents. Just remembering my uncle makes me want to kick his useless ass, or anyone's who mentions him."

Before he could punch Amjad's lights out, Laylah growled, "I swear, one more word out of either of you, and I'm putting each of you in a corner at the ends of this palace. *Ya Ullah*— now I remember why I left. I was drowning in male posturing and hormones. Are there any buffering women around here?"

"All the women who've invaded the Aal Shalaan male maze will be here tomorrow," Amjad said. "For today you can seek the feminine amelioration of my Maram, of course, and Johara."

She whooped. "I can't wait to meet the phenomenon who's put a collar around your neck. And see Johara again. And the children. You know, some sensible, age-appropriate-behaving individuals."

Amjad pulled another of those inciting expressions in his arsenal and shooed her away. "Skip along, then. Rashid and I have more juvenile silliness scheduled before we're through. I have to drive him to within an inch of his sanity before I even look into his application to acquire our last remaining—if long-stored and fraying around the edges—Aal Shalaan treasure."

Laylah grinned up at Rashid. "Guess you were right about my code name here." She turned her best demolishing glance on Amjad. "Not that anyone can accuse you of knowing how to hang on to your treasures, as evidenced by what happened to the Pride of Zohayd, your foremost one. So hang on to *your* sanity, Amjad. Rashid is a world-renowned authority in sanity extraction, among other…extractable things. I leave you to his not-so-tender mercies, *taal omrak.*"

Amjad let out a spectacular snort at her tagging the king's hail of "may you live long" to her irreverence. Then she stood on tiptoe and pressed a clinging kiss to Rashid's lips.

Before he forgot Amjad and the watchful eyes of the palace dwellers and crushed her to him, she drew away with a smile that lit his existence before almost dancing away.

Feeling bereft already without her, his gaze clung to her as she receded. And he registered where they were for the first time.

The royal palace of Zohayd was right up there with the Taj Mahal in splendor and intricacy of design, and even more extensive. The mid-seventeenth-century palace that had taken more than three decades and thousands of artisans and craftsmen to build had once been his playground and domain along with Haidar and Jalal from age eight to twenty. He'd taken as much pride and pleasure in it as they had before his stays here had declined until they'd stopped altogether, around ten years ago.

It felt so strange to be back after everything that had hap-

pened since to pollute his memory. Nostalgia was like a wave
that crashed down on him as he walked through this place
again, felt its history and the grandeur saturating its walls,
permeating his senses with bittersweet memories. On account
of its being Laylah's home, not the stage where chunks of his
life had been played. It had been mostly here where he'd seen
her and dared not dream of her. Now she was here *with* him. It
made being here again so…poignant.

Amjad, the self-appointed poignancy disperser, flicked a
hand at Laylah as she disappeared around a bend. "Are you as
viciously intelligent as you look? Did you latch onto Laylah
when you thought you were 'worthy' of her for the right reasons? Do you realize what a miracle she is? The product of Me-
dusa and Narcissus should have been a man-eating gorgon, not
the most sensitive, selfless being to walk the earth. That she's
female, too, makes her a veritable impossibility."

Now that Amjad was singing Laylah's praises, Rashid no
longer felt like wiping the palace floor with him face-first.

Still looking where Laylah had disappeared, as if to bask in
her echoes, he sighed. "Just what I was thinking. Before your
insufferable, inflammatory intrusion on our privacy."

"Insufferable, inflammatory intrusion? Can you say that
five times in quick succession?" Amjad suddenly slapped him
on the back. "So how did you do it?"

Struggling not to rearrange the king's well put-together face,
Rashid gritted, "Not choke you for all the insensitivities you
poured on Laylah's head? You're only still breathing because
I need you to do some talking on my behalf."

Amjad's guffaw was all enjoyment now. "I may like you yet."
Another back slap. "And by do it, I mean Laylah." At Rashid's
growl, Amjad held up his hands. "To quote Laylah, 'down boy.'
I *mean*—apart from her sharper-than-I-remember tongue—that
was a woman fathoms deep in love. I know the symptoms well.
My Maram looks and sounds like that around me."

"It must be the era of impossibilities."

Amjad laughed again. "Yeah, I still can't figure out why

Maram loves me. But I always figured Laylah's obsession with you stemmed from your unavailability. Now you're all over her, not to mention a far deteriorated version of your younger self. What's keeping someone like her interested in someone like you?"

"If you mean my scar…"

"Please. That's your one interesting feature. Provides you with character. Also proves you're human, since there have been major doubts about that. Nah, it has nothing to do with what you look like, and everything to do with what you *are* like. You're one dour, ruthless, unstable son of a bitch. Don't get me wrong, it makes you *my* kind of guy, but how can Laylah, that perpetual ray of sunshine, stand you?"

He forced out a breath. "How does your Maram stand *you?*"

"She does because we're alike. When you take away all the human traits I lack, she's got a razor for a mind and a scythe for a tongue, too. I don't believe in this opposites attract thing."

"Laylah and I are not opposites. We're very much alike, too."

Amjad snorted again. "Now I've heard it all."

"Think about it. As you pointed out, she is practically as parentless as I am. She has felt alone and out of place all her life, as I have. She's felt responsible for other people's crimes and punished herself for them."

"Her mother's crimes and your guardian's, huh? Now that you point it out, yeah, I can see the resemblance in all the major stuff." Amjad gave him an assessing glance. "So what's your real plan?"

Ten

Rashid's heart slammed against his ribs.

Amjad still suspected him? How, when he no longer *had* a plan?

He only had the truth to contribute. "I plan to dedicate my life to honoring her, to serving and championing her."

"Not to loving her?" Amjad tsked. "Women are fond of this part almost to the exclusion of all else."

And he did something he'd never thought he would: appealed to that maddening man. "You're a man in love, Amjad. Look at me and tell me you don't see *your* symptoms all over me."

After another protracted glance, Amjad let out a laugh. "And how. The trappings of *eshg*—extreme and unremitting love, though they clash on you like a pink dress on a grizzly bear— *are* all over you. But you have something against saying the words, right?"

"The words don't do justice to what I feel for her."

Amjad huffed again. "Been there, done that. And you'll invent new ways and words to transmit the enormity of your feelings. But those simple words, with the truth of your emotions behind them, have a way of transmitting exactly how you feel to your loved one. So word of advice—don't leave it too long without saying them, or she might have trouble getting comfortable hearing or believing them when you finally do."

It was Rashid's turn to scoff. "Now *I've* heard everything. You, giving me romantic advice?"

"That's for the cousin and sister who was the only beacon of brightness in this gloomy place for over two decades." Amjad suddenly made a hurrying gesture. "C'mon. Grovel already."

Giving Amjad a look that said he would make *him* grovel someday, Rashid said, "I ask that you gather the Aal Shalaan family tribunal to sanction giving me Laylah's hand in marriage."

A "gotcha" smile split Amjad's face. "You really are stuck in some desert knight folktale, aren't you? 'Tribunal', indeed."

Rashid counted to ten. "It's *your* family tradition."

"Tradition bladition. I'm King of Zohayd, pal. I play chess with those tribunal members. Just wait until I'm making them jump three diagonal moves ahead then back."

"So it's your decision that counts. *Zain.* Make your demands."

Amjad poked a finger at Rashid's temple, rapped it three times. "*Any* rudimentary sense of humor in there?"

Rashid swatted his hand away. "I'll snark your head off, *Ya Maolai,* as soon as Your Majesty approves my proposal. Or knock it off if you refuse it."

Amjad raised his arms up theatrically. "He lives!" One of his arms suddenly came around Rashid's shoulder, leading him toward the main palace hall. "Just because I now have hope that you won't bore Laylah to the point where she'd plot to be rid of you, I'll consider your proposal. But first, about those seven tasks…"

He knocked Amjad's arm off his shoulder. "No wonder your ex-wife tried to off you."

Amjad's grin was as unrepentant as ever. "She did when I had some propriety. Imagine what she would have done now."

"Shoot you, most probably."

"Is that what you feel like doing?"

"I would gladly kill anyone who would stand between me and Laylah. Or at least make him wish he was dead. Care to try?"

Amjad pretended horror. "You'll add me to your inventory of revenge? Will I tail the list after Haidar and Jalal?"

"Come between Laylah and I, and you'll reserve your spot at the top."

Amjad stuck his face into his. "You think you can take me?"

"I don't think. I know. And there wouldn't be much left of you once I'm done. And you know it."

Amjad's guffaw boomed again. "And he wins himself a doll."

"I swear, Amjad, if you don't stop yanking my chain, *taa omrak* won't be a concept that will apply to you anymore."

"You know, Rashid, I would have kicked you out on your ear with the first sign of kissing up. But you threatened to kill me instead, so I think I'm in love. Yep, rejoice. You passed." His arm was over Rashid's shoulder once more. "How about we go pretend that family 'tribunal' of mine actually matters?"

Still afraid to rejoice, Rashid hissed, "Didn't you say your word is everything, O king of all you survey?"

"It is. But you'll be king of the headache-inducing but inevitably inseparable Azmahar soon. You will be the one constant partner in my political bed. I'm doing myself a favor showing you the ropes of kingship. Yeah, I'm into training allies to my preferences. I'm charitable like that."

Rashid stilled. That was totally unexpected. That Amjad would bring up the idea of Rashid becoming king of Azmahar. And in this way. What was his game?

He probed, hoping to gain more insight. "It's strange that you'd assume I would be king with your two brothers running against me."

Amjad gave a dismissing wave. "Haidar and Jalal would make decent kings, I guess, but their hearts aren't really in it."

Yours is. You have more at stake in Azmahar and that is why you'll reap the votes."

Digesting this unforeseen development, Rashid put all his cards on the table, even if it was for a game he no longer cared about in the least. "I wouldn't without your alliance. Which *they* have in full."

Amjad gave a masterful imitation of affront. "Because they're my brothers? Nepotism? *Moi?* Tut-tut, shame on you. Have you forgotten they're only my *half* brothers? With Sondoss's blood running in their veins, actually half demon. Considering you're only half oaf, you win in that context, too."

Rashid looked heavenward. "Do you ever stop?"

"No. Maram won't let me."

Rashid tried one last time. "Are you *ever* serious?"

Those impossibly green eyes smoldered with a complex intelligence that had Rashid realizing this man saw and understood everything. "I'm *always* serious. I say what others are too shy or cowardly or merciful to say. Think back and you'll find I said nothing but the whole truth all through this bracing encounter." He clapped his hand once. "Now, from a full-fledged king to an embryonic one, let me give you an introductory course in dealing with pompous asses."

Rashid let Amjad put an arm around his shoulder this time. "You must be an authority on your own species."

Amjad chuckled. "I *can* still give you a hard time, you know."

"Knock yourself out. Name whatever price or mission. I'll surpass any so there won't be any shadow of owing you a thing."

"You can never repay what you'll owe me. Your eternal happiness with Laylah. Face it, Rashid. I own you."

He shrugged Amjad's arm off again. "Tell you what. Save it. I'll take Laylah up on her offer and elope."

Amjad's considering glance lengthened this time. "She's your Achilles' heel, isn't she?"

"You're all Greek mythology today, aren't you?"

Amjad gave a mock serious nod. "I've expended the Indian

and Middle Eastern myths on Haidar and Jalal in the past two days."

After that, Amjad remained miraculously silent as they passed through the majestic marble corridors adorned in the most intricate and magnificently designed colored mosaics toward the palace's great hall.

As they approached the hall's twenty-foot gilded double doors, Amjad suddenly spoke again, continuing his previous point seamlessly. "It balances you, grounds you, being so totally vulnerable to her." He winked. "It makes you a man at last." At Rashid's exasperated exhalation, Amjad added, "It's not a slur on your manhood. *This* time. I think a man can't call himself that until a woman has him totally whipped."

Unbelievable as it was, this Amjad was turning out to be one insightful and romantic fellow. "Like Maram has you?"

The smile that wreathed Amjad's face was the very essence of longing and indulgence, as if he was transmitting it to his wife. Rashid somehow believed Maram *would* feel it. "And then some. I gave up everything I had and was for her. I would give up far more if she'd let me. You'd do the same for Laylah, wouldn't you?"

"I would."

At his nonnegotiable answer, Amjad patted Rashid on the back as they entered the grand hall. "Then there's no rush with those seven tasks, Hercules. You'll be spreading them out throughout your lives together." He suddenly shuddered. "Just seeing her in labor is going to teach you the meaning of terror and take you to the limit of your endurance and beyond." They'd stopped in the middle of the expansive hall, below the hundred-foot central dome where Laylah's male kin were gathered in rows like a Roman senate, when Amjad gave him a playful punch. "You lucky bastard."

It was a marvel watching Amjad in action.

As he informed the Aal Shalaan elders that Rashid was going to marry Laylah, Amjad did the opposite of what kings, or anyone sane, should and had been known to do. In the past twenty minutes Rashid had watched him put down, make fun of and alienate everyone in the hall, including his father, in lieu of courting their favor. It was staggering how fluently and inventively he did it. But what was truly flabbergasting was that everyone loved him for it. They not only obeyed him, they practically invited him to walk all over them some more.

Maybe he should take private lessons in Amjad's School of Kingship, after all.

Suddenly, every thought in his mind dispersed as they walked out of the hall, only to be filled with one thing. Laylah.

She was striding toward him from the other end of the grand corridor, her dress's looseness only emphasizing her lethal curves, its cream color accentuating her sunlit hair, skin and eyes.

She had a taller woman with her. Maram, Amjad's wife and Queen of Zohayd. But though Maram's flawless complexion and silky hair approximated Laylah's hues, they didn't strike anything inside him like the burn of appreciation Laylah's did.

The moment it took to register Maram dissolved, everything gravitating to the center of his universe again. It struck him again how pleasurable it was to behold Laylah, how beautiful he found her. How terrified he was that this miracle wouldn't come to pass.

Suppressing the need to run to meet her halfway, he watched her and Maram approach, weighed down by the worry that kept ambushing him—that it would be impossible for everything to keep going so smoothly, incapacitating him further with each attack.

Maram flowed into Amjad's arms as if slotting into her other half. Then Laylah, flaunting tradition and inciting kingdom-wide wagging tongues, did the same with him. It was frowned upon for married couples to indulge in physical affection in public. It was unheard of between the unmarried.

Most likely presuming his stiffness was caused by his sense of propriety, Laylah grinned up at him. "Did those fossils agree to let you take me off the shelf or do I have to go in there and show them what the last remaining, if fraying around the edges, Zohaydan treasure will do if they snap her last decaying nerve?"

Maram groaned. "Those expressions reek of Amjad."

Laylah giggled. "Discipline him for me, will you?"

"It'll be my pleasure." Maram chuckled. "Though I suspect it will be his, too. I think he misbehaves on purpose."

Amjad pulled his wife deeper into his embrace. "Like any love-slave worth his salt, I live to provoke my next punishment."

As Maram laughed her pleasure, Laylah prodded him. "Well? Any need for drastic action on my side?"

Before Rashid got his constricted throat to work, Amjad produced the phone his *kabeer al yaweran*—his head of royal guard—had handed him as they'd exited the hall.

He gave it to Laylah. "I thought you should have an audio memento of me kicking our family's ass as I acquired for you the groom who's going to save you from a fate worse than death."

"You recorded the meeting?" Laylah exclaimed as she pounced on the phone and a chill assailed Rashid when she let him go. Then he once again heard the medley of abuse Amjad had exposed his family to. Amjad hadn't even introduced Rashid's proposal, had only pulverized everyone to their true size before announcing the upcoming marriage as a fact, and announcing that he'd be passing the royal decree documents for everyone to stamp with their house seal.

After gaping through the playback, Laylah squealed, "Amjad! You insane, incredible man, you!"

Amjad waved her delight away. "I don't do presents, so consider this my gift for the duration of your dual lifetimes."

Laylah gave him a squeezing hug. "Oh, Amjad, I love you!"

Amjad pushed out of her arms, a stern finger raised at her. "Don't do or say that again. And I mean *ever*."

Laylah winked at Maram. "Your mistress/owner will sanction the occasional hug from the universal kid sister around here."

Amjad's head jerk indicated Rashid, who'd taken an involuntary threatening step closer. "It's someone twice her size and who packs the wallop of a weapon of mass destruction that I'm worried about. Explaining this kid-sister thing to that monolith you brought home might not work. Or it might, and he'd still take my head off just because I'm male and you came in contact with me."

Laylah laughed, her whole face alight with elation as she looked up at Rashid. "Don't worry. He needs you in one piece."

Amjad tutted. "Not a good enough deterrent with that berserker. So let's play it safe." He pulled Maram back into his arms, shared with her that look of total allegiance that Rashid had unbelievably found with Laylah. "I have a wife and kids who'd like me around for half a century or so."

With the trio indulging in more banter, Rashid walked with them to Amjad and Maram's private quarters, still struggling with the ominous sensation settling deeper in his bones. It just didn't seem right that everything would go so wonderfully.

When would the other shoe drop?

It did, partially, in the evening.

More Aal Shalaans kept showing up to congratulate them, with their delight and acceptance only setting him further on edge. Then he announced the wedding would be in Azmahar a week later.

It was then that everything went wrong.

Maram and Aliyah led the women in insisting there was no way they'd put together another royal wedding in a week, like they recently had Jalal's. They'd take a month. And that was final.

When Amjad corroborated his wife's desire, and Laylah herself didn't protest for long, Rashid felt that if he did, they'd wonder why he was so nervous about postponement, and grudgingly succumbed.

From then on, he felt each moment as if it were counting down to an explosion that would go off and destroy everything.

Eleven

"You know, there's this age-old invention. It's said to have endless merits."

Rashid gritted his teeth as Laylah whispered in his ear. It had been ten days since they'd come to Zohayd. All the wedding preparations on the Zohaydan side had been concluded. They'd move to Azmahar in a couple of days to start the preparations there, where the ceremony would be held. A couple of days when Laylah wouldn't be with him.

She'd played a ruse on her companions to get him into her private quarters alone. Normally he would have objected, even refused. Not this time. He had to talk her out of her potentially disastrous decision.

He stiffened when her arms came around him from behind, her hair spilling its fragrant silk over his shoulder as she leaned over the couch where he sat in her old bedroom suite.

She nipped his earlobe. "That invention is called a smile."

Unable to hold back, he swung around, took hold of her and swept her over the couch and onto his lap.

Giggling, melting in his embrace, her fingers traced his tight lips, tried to spread them. "You do it like that. C'mon, you can do it. I promise you, your face won't crack."

He caught her hands. "It's not the right moment to ask me to try this trick."

Her face lost its impishness as she sighed. "I'm going to visit my mother, not going on a suicide mission."

"You mean there's a difference?" he asked, feeling himself spiraling out of control.

"You were the one who insisted I bring my family into this."

"I meant the nonvenomous ones only."

She chuckled. "I *am* one-quarter serpent."

"The gene bypassed you."

"But it might be a good idea to keep in touch with its literal mother lode, just to keep abreast of how to manage it. Said gene might not miss the next generation."

"It will. That gene stops with your mother and aunt."

She cupped his face in her hands. "And you know what? I almost believe you'd will that to happen."

"I would."

"You'll make an incomparable king, you know that?"

The fist around his heart squeezed. This subject of kingship had become the one thing he dreaded thinking or hearing about. "Let's not put me on a throne just yet." He caught her face in urgent hands, needing to defuse this catastrophe in the making. "Don't go, *ya rohi.* I don't want anything to poison your mood, *ya hayati,* not now, not ever."

She flushed in pleasure, her eyes filling with joy.

Amjad had been right. The words of love, as deficient as they were, had come to mean more, just because he said them to her, poured his emotions into them. She delighted in hearing him call her his soul and life. As she was.

After pressing a fiercely tender kiss on his lips, she withdrew. "It's why I'm going, *ya habibi.* Because there's this lingering bitterness that I want to get rid of. It will only go away if I see my mother again, talk this out with her." She sifted her fingers lovingly through the inch of hair he now had. "I also have this unstoppable need to brag that I not only amounted to something when left to my own devices, but I'm getting myself a husband worth millions of the men she tried to set me up with."

Struggling with the urge to bundle her up and hide her away, preferably forever, so nothing and no one could hurt her, he mumbled, "Icebergs will tumble in Azmahar's desert before she shares your opinion of me."

Her laugh tinkled over his overstrung nerves. "She might not admit it at peril of her life, but she must appreciate the hell out of what you are today, bless her power-hungry soul." She wrapped her arms around his neck. "But no matter what she's done to me, it *has* been her own misguided way of loving me. And no matter what she is, she's my mother...and I love her."

What could he possibly say to that? That she shouldn't give her mother any of her love because the woman didn't deserve it? When he didn't deserve it, either, yet wanted her to give him all the love she had?

He found himself groaning, "Don't go, if you love *me*."

He winced at how petty that had come out. How desperate.

She caressed his scar, deluging him in tenderness. "That's going to be a problem, since I don't 'love' you. You're just the sharer of my soul, and so far the owner of my heart."

His heart squeezed. "So far?"

"I'm assuming little Rashids will share your status one day."

The concept of children with her muted him.

Her touch ameliorated his upheaval, boosted it. "My mother won't attend our wedding, won't be able to practice her saboteur tricks. I'll see her in the safety of her exile and be back in less than forty-eight hours. And no, you can't come with me. I'm not so foolish that I'd put you in her range. And you have much to do. I know. I'm the one who set up your schedule."

He couldn't stop her without admitting what he would take to his grave. How this had started. And why he would prefer a worse scar than what he had to having her mother near her and therefore them, again.

So she'd go. And he'd spend forty-eight hours going insane. More insane than he already was.

He heaved to his feet, taking her up in his arms, rushing to her bathroom. "If you must go, then I must have you first."

"I should punish you for the celibacy you imposed on us," she teased as he locked the door. "But I'm just too hungry for you."

He took her lips, his tongue thrusting deep into her eager warmth. "Not as hungry as I am for you."

He dragged her down to a fluffy cream mat, tore her clothes out of the way, freed himself. He was heavy and hard and maddened for her molten depths. Ten days since he'd last been with her, inside her, had driven him to the edge.

He entered her in one full thrust, forging into the inferno of pleasure that was her welcoming flesh.

Her cries of pleasure drove him into a frenzy. He buried himself in her over and over, each plunge a shockwave of mindlessness from his loins to his every nerve.

Too soon the friction and ferocity drove them over the edge of insanity and into ecstasy. He poured himself into her depths, transfigured yet again with the power and totality of her desire, with the purity of passion she bestowed on him.

As she trembled and keened her satisfaction beneath him, blind possession overcame him. For a mad moment he wanted to force her not to leave him. He could keep her his willing prisoner...

Her lips opened over his scar, crooning his name, her love. Heat blossomed behind his eyes, burning away the instability.

Nothing would ever mean a thing if she didn't give it freely, breathlessly. He had to let her go.

As he took one last kiss, as if he could transmit his unspoken plea to never stop wanting him, he prayed.

That nothing would ever come between them.

Rashid had been right. She shouldn't have come.

Laylah was realizing that with every second. Her mother

was even more difficult than she'd remembered. Somayah's exile, though it was a luxurious one in Jamaica, had brought out the worst in her.

As majestic as ever, looking more beautiful than she remembered, her mother had received Laylah in full regalia, her hair blonder now but still in that signature chignon. She hadn't even pretended any pleasure to see her daughter, let alone to hear her news.

The news her mother had already known.

Somayah now looked down the four inches between them, disdain rising. "You think you'll…what? Impress me? Show me how you've succeeded against all my expectations? You think you did?"

Laylah's heart squeezed. She would have given anything to have what most people had. A mother who was on her side.

"My business is taking off, and I'm marrying the man who'll be your motherland's king. I'd say I did."

Her mother's glance grew more irritated. "You know what burns me? Since you were born, an Aal Shalaan female anomaly, I dedicated my life to making the most of this miracle, while trying to cure you of your Aal Shalaan defects."

Laylah's shoulders slumped further. "Yeah, you wanted to excise my Aal Shalaan half, turn me into a pure Aal Munsoori."

"I certainly wasn't after *that*. Though the Aal Munsooris are my father's house, the mundane, inept genes in our branch of the family are abundant. Just look at your uncle Nedal and his moronic sons. I always belonged body and soul to my mother's family and I wanted to polish you into an Aal Refa'ee gem. I wanted to raise you from the second-class princess I was to a queen. I worked tirelessly to plan you a marriage that would put you on a throne."

Laylah's lips twisted. "Then you should appreciate the irony here. Though you failed to set me up with those useless weasels whose only asset was their royal blood, I ended up with a man who will be king, because he deserves to be."

"There's irony in abundance here, indeed. For you to reject

all those men because they wanted you for your Aal Shalaan blood, only to *choose* a man who wants you for just that."

Laylah's heart stumbled. Her mother was assuming…

Of course, she was. She believed that blood was Laylah's only asset, believed everyone would think the same.

"But those men were honorable enough to declare their intentions. *This* leftover of the lowest branch of the Aal Munsooris, who is festering with hostility toward anyone higher than he is, is manipulating you, not even leaving you the dignity of knowing you are the chip he needs to become king."

Laylah's heart slowed down, as if afraid to take every next beat. "What—what are you talking about?"

Her mother's gaze grew incredulous. "I always knew you had no insight *or* foresight. But that you didn't even *suspect* him is too much. Let's review history, shall we? For your first seventeen years Rashid Aal Munsoori didn't look your way as you followed him around like a lost puppy, begging for a pat on the head." At Laylah's sharp intake of breath, her mother let out a bitter laugh. "Of course, I noticed. Everyone did. You were so obvious, it was painful to watch. That constituted the major part of my frustration with you. Especially as I watched him take his pleasure in pretending you didn't exist, and it only made you humiliate yourself more as you begged for smaller crumbs, until a glance your way was the height of your aspirations.

"Then, like all inferiority-complex-ridden breeds, the first thing he did once he could was bite the hands that offered him friendship and support. He did everything he could to destroy your kin, but being the pathetic thrall that you are, I bet you convinced yourself he must have good or even noble reasons."

"You know nothing about him, in the past or now."

"I know far more than you do, you stupid girl. Didn't you even ask yourself why, after you lived without incident in the United States, you were suddenly targeted for kidnapping? When you were no longer a good candidate for ransom, with half your family in exile and the other half off the royalty A-list? Didn't you wonder how he happened to be there to save you?"

Her mother's insinuations sank into her brain. "No…"

Her mother barreled on. "Let me guess what happened next. You were so grateful for his saving you, so thankful for the opportunity to be with him, you clung to him. Did he pretend to reciprocate your feelings right off, or did he dangle the bait of reluctance to stir you into a frenzy? How long did he make you pant after him before he deigned to let you closer? Knowing you, I expect you offered him everything, if only he'd take it. And he ended up taking it all, didn't he?"

Suddenly her legs lost all cohesion. Laylah collapsed on the nearest couch, feeling like the little girl who used to suffocate under the barrage of her mother's censure. But the way her mother wielded her contempt now was beyond any cruelty she'd inflicted on Laylah before.

And she wasn't done. "So how soon did he play his hand? Ask to marry you? I expect he made you sweat it first." That was the only part her mother had gotten wrong. It was as if she'd been with them, only putting alternate, horrifying interpretations on the actual events. "You didn't find any of what was happening strange? That after a lifetime of shoving your irrelevance in your face, and after he declared war on your family, he'd explode into your life out of the blue and risk his life for yours? Then, in record time, ask to marry you? What reason did he give for this? What's the reason *you* told yourself? That he wants you for you, not like all those 'weasels' you so righteously and shrewdly rejected?"

Mute with pain, coming apart with dread, that her mother still had worse to say, Laylah stared helplessly up at her.

"Let me tell you why he's swallowing your abhorred pill," her mother hissed. "Because you're the only remedy for a major ailment he has. A severe lack of Aal Shalaan blood. Only a blood bond with the king of Zohayd through marriage will put him on the throne of Azmahar. And the only available female Aal Shalaan is you."

That "you" felt like a direct hit to Laylah's heart.

Her mother bent over her as if to make every word a harder blow. "But he couldn't come to you with a proposition to use you to forge an alliance with Zohayd. Knowing you, you would have agreed to anything he asked, but he probably couldn't risk the Aal Shalaans, especially that paranoid madman Amjad, suspecting his motives. So he had to make you think this was real. Since he knows everything about you and your infatuation with him, a little act was all he needed to have you thanking fate for bringing him into your life and blindly swallowing his bait. As you did."

"Please…stop…"

At her bleeding whisper, her mother straightened. "I have nothing more to add. You can now go sacrifice yourself at the altar of your obsession with this psychopath, let him step on you to the throne of Azmahar then kick you aside once he sits on it. Or maybe he'll keep you until he uses your womb to create a permanent source of Aal Shalaan blood, one he actually wants."

Laylah stared at her mother, wounded to her core that Somayah would think nothing of mutilating her own daughter to "cure" her of her "obsession" with Rashid. But…what if anything she'd said was true…?

No. It wasn't. It couldn't be…

Her mother interrupted her chaotic thoughts. "Go ask him, Laylah. Look into his eyes as you ask, as he answers. If you're certain in your heart that nothing I said is true, then just forget about it."

With that, her mother turned, leaving the cloud of her exclusive fragrance behind as she exited the room.

Impending loss consumed Laylah. Whatever the outcome of confronting him, she'd lose something vital irrevocably. If her mother turned out to be wrong, Laylah wouldn't forgive her, losing her forever.

If her mother was right, Laylah would lose everything else.

Twelve

"What's your game this time, Rashid?"

He groaned at the sound of that voice. Haidar. His once-best friend. Rashid hated him now as much as he'd once loved him.

But he had no time to continue their battles. The pilot of his private jet had said he'd be landing in an hour. Rashid had to be at the airstrip to meet Laylah. She'd said not to come, that she'd be at the palace in half an hour. But he could not wait a half hour longer to see her.

He turned toward Haidar. He was blocking the door of Rashid's suite in Azmahar's royal palace where he'd be staying while the wedding preparations were being made.

His careless glance answered Haidar's black scowl as he passed him on his way out of the room. "Schedule a duel with Ahmad on your way out, Haidar."

His arm was snagged in Haidar's grip. "Is marrying Laylah part of your war on us?"

Rashid swung around to face Haidar, snarling. "She has *nothing* to do with any of that."

"So what will you have me believe?" Haidar hissed. "That you fell in love with her and that's why you're marrying her?"

He shook off Haidar's hand. "I care nothing about what you believe. Will you see yourself out, or do you need help?"

Haidar blocked his way again, furious, urgent, entreating. "Whatever it is you think you have against me and Jalal, do whatever you want to us. *We* can take it. But Laylah has always loved you, and if you're using her, it will destroy her."

"You think I need to use anyone to trounce you?"

"Then is this about the throne? If you're trying to complete the last corner in your campaign through her, I'll save you the trouble. I'll make the battle unnecessary. I'll withdraw from the race. I can make Jalal do the same. Just don't do this to her."

Something snapped inside him. He hefted Haidar off the floor, slammed him into the wall, a beast's snarl issuing from his depths. "I will say this once, Haidar. I have always wanted Laylah, but now I find no reason and no way to exist without her. I would rather die, or worse, than hurt her. So if you dare insinuate otherwise, I won't fight you anymore, I'll finish you."

Haidar's fingers dug into his hands hard enough to penetrate his red haze of aggression, extricating himself from his rabid grasp, his eyes narrowing, as if to gauge Rashid's sincerity.

Seeming convinced, Haidar exhaled. "With you turning all Comte De Monte Cristo on us, I feared there might be no line you wouldn't cross. I also thought you'd never fall in love. *B'Ellahi,* the only girlfriend we ever heard about turned out to be fictional. For years you misled us into thinking you picked that inferior college to be near said girlfriend, not because it was what you could afford. And then, Laylah kept trying to get you to notice her, and you never showed any indication you even saw her."

"Just as I couldn't afford a better college, I couldn't afford to look at her." His heart convulsed. "I still can't believe I have her now."

Exasperation filled Haidar's face. "This pride of yours— this pathologically huge sense of honor—it stopped you from taking everything that was yours. Our support, Laylah's love. And it made you saddle yourself with your bastard of a guardian's debts, so that you derailed your whole life to pay them off, without help from anyone."

"But when I *really* needed help, and it clashed with your best interests, you didn't care if I lived or died." At Haidar's bewildered glance, he plowed on. "So don't think I will spare you now because you're Laylah's cousin."

Still looking confused, Haidar smirked. "Not even if she asks you to? If you love her as much as you claim, you'll do whatever she wants. Like I would, for Roxanne."

"I am bound to obey her, even if it means my honor and my life. But if she does ask, I might tell her the truth about you. She would withdraw her intervention if she knew what you did."

Haidar exploded. "And what the hell *did* I do, damn you?"

"You damned *me*."

At his bellow, Haidar's stupefaction felt real.

Was it possible Haidar didn't know what Rashid was referring to?

No. No time to dwell on the possibility of anything this disturbing, this huge. He had to get to Laylah. Only she mattered.

He pushed past Haidar, making it clear there would be no detaining him this time. "Now my salvation is waiting for me, and you're keeping me from her. I'd decimate you for that alone."

The moment he cleared the door, his heart stopped.

Laylah. A dozen feet from his door.

After the first drench of unreasoning horror that she might have heard anything, he ran to sweep her into his arms.

"Habibati..." he groaned against her temple, her cheeks, her lips. "How are you here already?"

"We landed earlier."

"And Zaaher didn't tell me!"

"At my insistence, so don't you dare take this up with him."

His heartstrings vibrated with the delight of having her in his arms again. *"To'moreeni*—as you command."

"It's creepy how you have Rashid doing your bidding, Laylah." Haidar stopped by their side, dropped a kiss on her head and met Rashid's incensed gaze with a calm glance. Rashid's fury rose as Laylah returned Haidar's smile and kiss. "It's like seeing a shark doing tricks in a swimming pool. Who knew you had it in you? But keep up the good work, *ya bent al amm.* Holding the reins of such an unstoppable force can come in handy. For us."

Rashid bit back something demolishing. He'd never expose her to tension. Which might mean sparing Haidar and Jalal, after all.

He'd think about that later. All he could think of now was that he had her back.

Uncaring anymore that the palace dwellers would see him taking her to his quarters, the moment she said goodbye to Haidar, he rushed back there with her in his arms. He told himself he'd never let her go again.

Laylah clung to Rashid as if she'd never let him go, feeling reclaimed from the hell of doubts and dread.

Before she could say anything, he opened his mouth on her neck, suckled her as if assimilating her into himself, growling those extravagant endearments he'd been deluging her in of late.

Fireworks exploded in her blood as he put her down, ground the steel of his erection into her belly, showing her she only had to wrap herself around him and he'd fill her emptiness.

She forgot everything but this, him, them, like that.

"Rashid, take me…"

At her urgency, he snatched her dress up, spreading her thighs around his hips. He pressed her against something that rattled as he freed himself, tore her panties out of the way then slid her up to scale his length. She felt the hot hardness of him at her entrance, keened, disintegrating with the firebomb of hunger he'd detonated inside her. Obeying her plea for hard and fast, he let her crash down on him as he thrust up, impaling her.

It took no more than feeling him inside her—filling her beyond her capacity, embedding at the gate of her womb—to shatter her. She screamed as an orgasm unleashed all her tension, squeezed her around him inside and out.

Igniting with her, he fed her convulsions with thrust after thrust, mingling his growls with her shrieks. "*Aih, khodeeni kolli, eeji alai*—take all of me, come all over me."

Pleasure raged on until he roared and slammed into her, the pulse of his release wringing her of sensations. She sobbed, her flesh quivering around him.

Possessing her slack mouth, he filled her breathless lungs with his ragged breath, rocking gently inside her, satisfying her to her last tremor.

"*Awhashteeni...bejnoon...*"

I missed you...insanely...

Her head flopped on his shoulder as she tried to get her nerves to spark. She needed to hold on to his reality, his magic, to ward off the doubts. "It's been...less than...two days."

"*Kateer. Tw'hasheeni wenti gossad aini.*"

Too much. I miss you when you're right before my eyes.

Could all this...sincerity be a lie?

He strode with her wrapped around him to the bathroom. He lowered her gently on pristine white marble before reluctantly, carefully, withdrawing from her depths.

She moaned at his beauty and caring as he kneeled in front of her, taking care of the evidence of their lovemaking. Then he rose to his feet, muscles rippling under his shirt as he struggled to stuff his erection into his pants, his emotions an open book for her to read in his eyes.

But how could *that* be the truth? The mainstay of Rashid's character was his reticence. How could he have become so... uninhibited? Because of her overwhelming effect on him? Or because it was easy to say and pretend what he didn't feel?

Which explanation sounded more plausible?

The answer, validated by the evidence of history, was so incontrovertible, her stomach heaved. The dream she'd been living in quivered on the verge of plunging into a nightmare.

It was no use trying to ignore this. Doubt was poisoning her, snuffing out her life. She had to know for sure.

What if he denied it? Would she ever feel secure again? Would the doubts ever go away?

Yes. They would. Her mother had no idea who Rashid was. She was projecting her own end-justifies-the-means beliefs on him.

Rashid would tell her the truth. And she'd believe him.

She urged his head up as he rained kisses and words of worship all over her face and neck.

His glazed-with-passion, heavy-with-indulgence eyes met hers.

Feeling like she was about to jump off a cliff, she asked, "Do you need to marry me to become king of Azmahar?"

His face shut down. But not before she saw it.

The alarm. The dismay. Of premature exposure.

Everything her mother had said was true.

Rashid stared at Laylah, feeling his heart had burst.

So this was it. What he'd been dreading. The catastrophe that would end everything.

Every shred of control he'd been struggling for years to muster suddenly drained away. The chaos that was always hovering at the edge of his awareness crashed into his mind, unraveling it…

No. He couldn't afford to surrender to the volatility that threatened to swallow him whole. He had to contain this.

Then he opened his mouth, and his voice sounded like he felt, desperate, out-of-control. "Is…is that what your mother told you?"

Her eyes, for the first time ever, were a void, expressing nothing. "I want *you* to tell me."

His hands dug into her shoulders, feeling if he didn't cling to her, she'd disappear. "I don't care about the throne anymore. I only care about you. You must believe that."

He had no idea if that helped or hurt his case. There was nothing in her expression to guide him.

"But it's true that, no matter if you're the best candidate, without an alliance with Zohayd, you won't claim the throne?"

She needed the truth, and he'd give it to her. He'd explain how things had started, how they'd changed. She'd understand.

Maybe it was for the best this had come out, so he'd stop self-consuming with worry, so total disclosure would leave no possibility for anything going wrong or coming between them.

He still couldn't breathe due to anxiety. "Azmaharians believe they need Zohayd's alliance to survive. I always believed this dependence on Zohayd was toxic, and intended to make Azmahar fully independent if I became king. But I was left in no doubt that to become king I had to form a connection with Zohayd. The only way I could rival Haidar's and Jalal's blood relation to Zohayd's king was to form one of my own with him."

"And the only way was through marriage." Her voice was as expressionless as her face. "Since I am the closest thing Amjad has to a sister, and I happen to be the only available female Aal Shalaan, anyway, you had no choice but to marry me."

Hearing her analyze the plan he'd once weaved turned his stomach. And that was before she went on.

"So you planned to hunt me down, pretend you didn't find me as abhorrent as you did my family and con me into marriage. Once you impregnated me and your heir replaced me as a perpetual blood bond, you'd discard the worthless creature you believed me to be."

The accuracy of her projections drenched him with desperation. "Whatever I thought or planned, everything changed from that first night. That first *hour*."

A faraway look came into her eyes, as if she was looking back into that time. "It was no coincidence that you were there that night. I felt your presence for weeks before that." His choking silence corroborated her assumption. "You were studying me, like a hunter would his prey, finding out my habits, my haunts, to use this knowledge and my obliviousness to get to me. Once you made 'accidental' contact, you used the data you gathered to manipulate me into entering your trap willingly, even eagerly. As I did."

Hot needles invaded his heart. "That was true, until you were attacked. Everything changed from then on. *Everything.*"

"You mean the attack you planned? The rescue you enacted?"

He almost doubled over with her accusation.

This was beyond his worst fears. That she'd think…think…

Her next words had protests recoiling in his chest, hacking into it. "The ironic thing is, you didn't need to set me up. If you, of all people, had offered me a marriage of convenience, I would have jumped at the opportunity. That was how much I wanted you. I would have agreed to your cold deal and dreamed of one day melting your heart, of making you see me as more than a means to your end. I would have probably realized the mistake I had made sooner rather than later, but you would have gotten what you wanted by then. Just think about it—the truth would have served your purpose far better than this charade."

"There was no charade," he groaned, desperation taking over. "Every moment with you was the only real thing I ever had…"

Her eyes suddenly filled with tears, suffocating him. "But you couldn't risk my family, especially Amjad, suspecting your motives, so you had to make me believe in your authenticity. But even with an heir binding you forever to the Aal Shalaans, you wouldn't have risked a falling-out with them when you discarded me." Her reddened eyes seemed to melt. "Did you plan another attack to get rid of me after I'd served my purpose?"

He'd taken a bullet in the gut before. He'd been showered in shrapnel. He'd been tortured beyond the limits of endurance and sanity. Her projections hurt, damaged him, far more.

He couldn't even shout his denial, could only choke his horror. "*Ya Ullah ya Laylah, laa*—don't even utter such ugliness…"

Those eyes that had bathed him in the balm of their belief, drilled into him now with bitterness and betrayal. "Ugliness is what you did to me, what you plunged me into. Now I'll never feel anything untainted by its sordidness again."

Disintegrating with the need to ward off the pain he'd inflicted on her, he extended a trembling hand to her. "You won't believe anything I say now, but when you're over the first rage and disillusion, remember what we shared…"

"We shared *nothing.*" Her voice was thick with disdain. "Nothing but your deceit and exploitation. But I can't even blame you. I'm the one who threw myself at you. You only obliged and jerked me around. I deserve everything you did to me."

And it was as if a dam broke. Sobs racked her body, tears ran in torrents down her cheeks.

"Y-you want me to remember? I *do.* Every thought and emotion as I loved you…craved you…and longed to be there for you. Every sensation as I touched you…as you touched me, moved inside me…until I felt you were part of me. How you must have despised me for…how easy I was, how cheaply I came…"

Her pain crushed his heart.

But his pain didn't matter. Only hers did. He wanted to absorb her agony.

At his imploring touch, she tore herself away, quaking on sobs he feared would tear her insides apart. "I spent my *whole life* looking up to you… I thought you were made of honor, of integrity…that if there was a haven in this world for me… it would be you. But not even those who I thought would have raped and killed me could have…*debased* me like you did."

He fell to his knees before her, insanity clawing at his mind, begging. "Don't let pain take you that far, *ya habibati,* I beg you. Rage and rave and slash me apart…but don't make me a demon when I'm only a pathetic fool. I did devise the plot, but I didn't see it through…"

"You did," she wailed. "That first night—*ya Ullah*—how did you *do* it? Anticipating me…adjusting your response on the fly to keep me hurtling…deeper into your trap. You had me in your bed in hours…thinking it was at my insistence. You stayed up

all night, didn't you? It was the only time you forced yourself to stay beside me…burning to close the deal. You must have wanted to strangle me when I…forced you to pretend to court me before I returned with you to Zohayd so ecstatic, I managed to fool…even Amjad for you. You would have seen it through to the end…if I hadn't found out the truth."

"That's *not* the truth." His protest strangled as she stumbled away from his begging hands only to collapse a foot away, ending up with her streaming face pressed against the wall, her whole body quaking. "But whatever else you think me guilty of, I beg you, believe I had nothing to do with the attack."

"Do you know that my earliest memory is of you?"

He doubled over with the surprise confession.

Her sobs subsided by degrees. "It was my fourth birthday. You were standing behind Haidar, wearing light blue jeans and a black T-shirt. I thought you were the most wonderful thing I'd ever seen. As I blew out the candles I made one wish, for you to be my friend. I've made no other wish since.

"I idolized you, saw a wealth of beauty in everything about you, even the way you kept your distance. I thought we shared so much, both of us outsiders, with no one who loved us most or put us first. I lived dreaming of our being each other's allies against all odds. Now all my memories are contaminated with the truth, and my past wasted in loving a figment of my imagination. My future will be consumed in regret over every moment and emotion I wasted on you."

He crawled toward her, the ground burning him worse than the sands he'd once dragged himself over for days to a salvation that kept receding. Her feeble resistance died as his arms shook around her, taking her drenched face against his heaving chest.

"Don't say that…don't think it and make it real in your mind. Don't do this to yourself, to us. I *never* lied about my feelings…"

Her head rolled against his shoulder, her eyes meeting his. For seconds he saw his Laylah, felt he might reach her again.

Then she whispered, "I would have laid my life down for you, Rashid. Now I would rather die than see you again."

She pushed away from him, stumbled up to her feet.

Looking down at him as he remained on his knees, demolished, her eyes were as dead as her voice. "Wishing you the heartbreak you inflicted on me wouldn't work when you have no heart. So I'll settle for crippling you like you crippled me. I'll make sure you lose the only thing that matters to you—the throne."

Thirteen

"So how *did* you manage to lose that girl?"

Amjad's sarcasm scraped across Rashid's every screaming nerve.

He turned slowly toward Amjad. He'd been doing everything slowly since he'd followed Laylah back to Zohayd less than a day after she'd left him in Azmahar. Any sudden moves might set him off.

His trigger quivered as Amjad sauntered toward him from his office on the ground floor of the royal palace of Zohayd, his signature mockery hitting him between the eyes.

"You must have committed some nuclear-level stupidity to blast through her immutable worship of you."

"Listen, *King* Amjad," he snarled. "I have only been in anything approaching this state once in my life. I was cut open and my life was bleeding out. And I still managed to kill all my torurers. There were eight of them. I am now far more desperate."

"Whoa. Are you aware you just threatened to kill a king right in his own palace? Or are you really as out of it as you look?"

"That threat is a few more words from becoming reality.

And don't think your royal guard can help you. I can end you all without breaking a sweat."

"You know what?" Amjad gave him the once-over. "I believe you can, Super Soldier-man. But what next? You massacred your previous tormenters, who I assume gave you this delightful souvenir—" he flicked a hand at Rashid's scar "—and escaped to live long and prosper. I don't see a similar scenario here, as there'll be no living long and prospering for you now. Not without Laylah."

Hearing her name slipped another notch of his control. "I am at the point where I don't care what happens next. If you don't get out of my way, I'll kill you for the pleasure of it."

Amjad smirked. "Was that why Laylah canceled your wedding? She discovered your homicidal tendencies?"

Rashid didn't even try to hide the truth. "She believes I want to marry her only to have an alliance with Zohayd. With *you*."

"That's not true. Sure, being Laylah's husband will sweeten the deal when I take you under my wing. But that's just collateral damage. You really love her."

"Love? Love is a conditional emotion tainted with self-serving. I've been using the word, making believe it means what I feel. But I can't describe how I feel for Laylah. There is right and wrong and honor and disgrace, until it comes to her. Then there is only her. There's nothing I wouldn't do, nothing I wouldn't endure or sacrifice for her."

Amjad held up his hands. "Hey, I'm not the one you should swing that sales pitch at. *I* believe you. It takes one colossal fool for love to know another. I almost alienated Maram forever, too. Good news is, those women of ours love once and all the way, no matter what. Yeah, Maram told me as much, after she nearly killed me, before taking me back. So even if you think your world is over and Laylah lost to you forever, if you grovel creatively enough, strip yourself to the bone until there's not much left, she'll relent, fish you out of hell and dunk you back in paradise."

Amjad's assurances did nothing to dispel Rashid's despair

"Maram discovered you used her to get the Pride of Zohayd jewels back. But your goal looked noble, as the conspiracy could have resulted in war. Laylah discovered I planned our engagement to become king, which looks purely self-serving. And while you kidnapped Maram under the pretext of a sandstorm, Laylah believes I approached her under the pretext of a kidnapping attempt."

Amjad scowled. "Okay, that's where you not only lose all my sympathy, it's where I might have you thrown in the dungeon. I might even let you sit on that throne just to squash you on it."

"If you think me capable of something like that, feel free to treat me like the criminal it would make me."

After a contemplative second, Amjad waved. "Nah. One thing I'm infallible at is reading people. Especially men. You have some terminally honorable syndrome, wouldn't scare any woman like that, not even for a throne. So, where did she get the idea?"

"Hasn't she already told you everything?" he gritted.

"She informed us the wedding was off, wouldn't be persuaded to say why, adding only that she never wanted to see you again."

This bewildered him. "She said she would stop me from becoming king. I thought she would tell you what she believes happened, ending any chance of an alliance between us. Why didn't she carry out her threat?"

Amjad's lips twisted. "See? A sign that she still cares."

"I know how much she cares—*cared*. Her agony and disillusion now is as absolute."

"Yeah, I know." At his exasperated growl, Amjad tsked. "Seems I'm going to have a perpetually pissed off lion for an ally."

"You won't have *anything* if you keep condescending to me."

"No condescension. *This* time. I told you, been there, done that, with Maram." Amjad grinned. "Tell you what. I'll work on Laylah. I'll exasperate her until she has to talk to you again."

The hope that Laylah might speak to him again caused Rashid's throat to almost close. "You'd do that for me?"

"Yep. I'm magnanimous like that."

"You get her to speak to me again, Amjad, and I'll hand you my neck on the end of a leash."

Amjad winked at him. "*That's* how I like my allies. Done."

Then with one more smirk, Amjad turned and walked away.

Rashid watched him leave, thoughts of tearing through the palace looking for Laylah roiling like thunderclouds through his mind.

But what would he do when he found her? She was no longer his Laylah, but the woman who'd told him no one had hurt or degraded her like he had. What could he do to atone?

Before he could make a move, Haidar and Jalal exploded through the palace doors. He watched them stride toward him, their steps and expressions laden with fury.

Haidar almost slammed into him, did punch him in the chest "You lied to me."

Jalal wrenched him around. "You did plan to use her to get the throne, didn't you?"

Haidar jerked him back. "And you're here looking like a madman, to what? Beg for Amjad to *still* endorse you for the throne of Azmahar? Yeah, we know he thinks you're the number one candidate. That weasel. But he turned out to be a stupid one. You had even him fooled."

Rashid shoved the twins away. "You two and the throne can go to hell. I'd send you all there if I had time for you. But I don't."

He stormed away. Haidar and Jalal caught up with him on the first floor, dragged him into an empty meeting room.

"You're not walking away from us again," Haidar hissed.

"We're getting everything out in the open once and for all. Jalal turned from closing the door. "And I mean *everything*."

Images of cutting them both down where they stood, something he could do in his sleep, deluged his mind.

Suppressing the mindless aggression with the last tatters of control, he glared at them. "You're still pretending you don't know why I hate you? You're still trying to slither your way out of any responsibility, you sons of a serpent?"

"Shut up, you exasperating son of a…" Haidar jerked his shoulders uneasily. "I have no idea what your mother was, but I sure as hell won't call her names so I can insult *you*."

"Calling your mother a serpent is a terrible insult—" he bit off "—to the worst human snake who ever lived. But you want my version of what happened? So you can have a complete picture? Fine."

And with four years' worth of anger and agony and betrayal churning up his insides, he told them.

As they gaped at him throughout his account, one thing became indisputable. They *hadn't* known.

They'd had no hand in what had been done to him.

He'd lived for years poisoned by the belief that they'd brutally betrayed him, for nothing.

Finally, a shell-shocked Haidar said, "*Ya Ullah ya* Rashid—you spent all these years thinking we did that to you? And we're still in one piece?"

Jalal, seeming as stunned, nodded. "That's what I'm wondering, too. That you believed what you did, and only tried to destroy us in business, gives me a whole new insight into your character. You must be part saint."

Rashid couldn't bear another word. "I don't care about what happened or who did it or why anymore. I only care about Laylah."

Haidar approached him tentatively. "But if you tell her what you just told us, she'd—"

"No." His shout went off like a gunshot. "She will *never* hear anything about this. I'm not getting her back at this price."

Jalal approached from the other side, as if helping his twin contain the volatile quantity that was Rashid. "It might be the only price that's good enough, Rashid."

"I said *no.* And if you tell her, I will stop at nothing this time to punish you for breaching my confidence."

Haidar ventured a hand on his shoulder. "Settle down, will you? We won't say a thing." He squeezed his eyes. "*Ya Ullah*— what I really want is to wipe everything you said from my mind. But then, a mental scar is nothing compared to what you suffered."

Any other time, Rashid might have felt relief that the scar of losing them would heal, that he could have them back in his life and heart. But now that he no longer had Laylah there, nothing meant anything.

Haidar leveled his gaze on Rashid, anguish and regret gripping his face. "I can't tell you how powerless I feel that I can neither change the past nor punish the culprits. But I will put this right if it takes the rest of my life. You're my other twin, Rashid, and I've been…bereft all these years without you. I swear to you, we'll make up for lost time."

Jalal joined his twin in his pledge. "That goes for me, too. But you're right, Rashid. What matters now is Laylah. I swear to you, we'll do everything to reunite you with her."

Everything hadn't been enough.

It had now been eighteen days in a hell worse than anything he'd known, sinking deeper in the quicksand of Laylah's rejection.

Amjad had given him quarters close to hers so he could "stalk" her, or they'd do a "pincer" on her, with everyone herding her toward him until she was forced to confront him.

She didn't. She'd let them push her to within inches of him only to pass him by as if he didn't exist. A punishment for his present transgressions and past avoidance. Feeling nonexistent to her, no matter if it was on purpose, was excruciating.

So he'd written his confessions in what had amounted to a small volume, which had been fated to the bin.

And he'd been forced to do what he'd thought impossible.

He'd poured his heart out to anyone who'd listen. That ultimate exposure *had* felt like he'd "stripped himself down to the bone" as Amjad had said. Not that it had any effect.

She'd treated the explanations everyone transmitted with the same disdain she had his written ones. She'd had to grudgingly believe he hadn't orchestrated the attack on her, under the deluge of proof he'd provided. But she believed his withdrawal from the race for the throne to be another convoluted plan to gain more sympathy and strengthen his position.

He'd hit rock bottom when he'd realized how completely she'd lost her faith in him.

"There is no line you won't cross, is there?"

His whole being seized in shock. In delight. Laylah. Here. His heart boomed so hard it swung him around to her.

"Laylah…"

She was closing the suite's door and turning to him, indescribable in a floor-length silk turquoise dress that offset the perfection of every inch of skin it didn't cover, intensified the burnished gloss of her hair.

Brutal longing paralyzed him as she stopped two feet away, her eyes those of a stranger.

"It was almost embarrassing, watching how far you went in 'exposing' your 'inner self' in your damage-control efforts. But what really surprises me is how totally you've taken my family in. I thought they, especially Amjad, were shrewd. I guess no one is immune to your powers of emotional manipulation."

"They are shrewd people," he rasped. "That's why they recognize my sincerity against all damning evidence."

Her laugh was mirthless. "You know, I was delusional to think someone with your life experiences had any emotions left. Logically, you can't be faulted for that. The first thing you must have learned in order to deal with your personal situation, then your life as a soldier, was to turn off your emotions. It only makes sense that you feel nothing but ambition and hunger for power now."

He reached an aching hand to the thick lock of hair undulating over her breast. "If only that was true."

She stepped away, making the silk slip through his fingers just as she kept doing. "Please, stop the pretense. I'm not angry at you anymore." She wasn't? "Actually, most of my anger was directed at myself. For believing what I so fiercely wanted to believe. Nothing you did ever added up, but I was so desperate for you, I silenced my disbelief that you could fall for me at all, let alone that fast, that you'd tie yourself to me for life. Disillusion and damage were the only possible outcome for my stupidity."

He took her by the shoulders, wouldn't let her shake him off this time, his grip gentling until she let him hold her.

"Laylah, you have to listen to me. Not so that I can beg your forgiveness or exonerate myself. You need to listen for *you*. What pains me most is that this has reinforced your belief that no one has ever wanted you for you, when the reverse is true. You are valued and loved by everyone who knows you. You are worshipped by me. Even if you choose to never forgive me, please be secure in that, and that my crimes are a reflection on me, never on you."

For a long moment, as the setting sun struck russet in eyes that gazed at him as if realizing something profound, he started to hope that at least he'd succeeded in this endeavor.

Then they filled with cool disdain as she removed his hands with utmost tranquility. "That's your latest strategy? Feed my need for validation and heal my fractured self-image? Sorry, but I've beaten you to it. I've come to terms with the fact that my worth has nothing to do with how others see it, starting with my parents and ending with the queue of men like you. value me. If others don't, no matter who they are, screw them."

"I'll do anything to solidify your certainty. Ask for the impossible, impose any punishment…"

"It's me who'll be punished. When I marry you."

Was his mind disintegrating at last? He'd thought he heard her say…

"I've already told my family that the wedding is on again.

He could only stare at her.

"I'm pregnant."

Power drained from his body, coherence from his mind,
beats from his heart.

The wall suddenly slammed into his back. He'd staggered
under the blow of shock. Of joy. And grief. At the way she'd said
it. As if it was the worst thing that had ever happened to her.

"Laylah, *habibati*..."

She warded off his embrace. "I'm not sharing the happy
news with my adoring groom, I'm informing my ingenious
manipulator that your plan has worked to the last detail."

"It was *not* a plan—"

"I don't care what you call it. But you were not only right
in predicting the outcome of me 'shredding your ironclad control,' but in anticipating what I'd do, even if I discovered your
plot prematurely. You knew me well enough to realize that
even if I kept saying I don't care about my family, I do. Even if
I don't care about tradition, they do. Especially when it comes
to legitimacy. I won't impose illegitimacy on my baby, when
there's a father so eager to put his claim on it, even for all the
wrong reasons."

Could he have destroyed her love so absolutely he'd become
so unredeemable in her eyes?

Her cold stare said he had and was. "Go ahead, Rashid,
don't struggle to keep a straight face. Your charade is out in
the open and it won't hurt your agenda anymore to celebrate
your success. An Aal Shalaan blood bond, and after the masterful lovelorn, honorable knight act you plied my family with,
a sure path to the throne of Azmahar. If the baby turns out to
be male—and I bet it will, since you seem to will fate to obey
you—you'll even get the heir you need right away."

"None of this has any truth to it anymore."

"The only truth here is that history is repeating itself. I was
the result of a toxic marriage of convenience and I swore no
child of mine would ever suffer anything like that. And here I
am, repeating my parents' terrible pattern. But I'll be damned if
I'll live a life filled with hostility and resentment. I'll play into
your hands willingly. I will give you the one thing you wanted

from me and suffer through this wedding, *only* so that it will legitimize the baby in our society's eyes. This ordeal will assure that our baby gets all its rights from you, no matter what happens, so after we announce my pregnancy and convince people the baby was conceived within wedlock, this travesty of a marriage ends."

Leaving him suffocating on her rejection again, she turned and walked away. The need to rush after her, catch her back, kiss her and melt her almost had him roaring.

Two things held him back. Knowing that he could swear and beg and produce a thousand proofs, and she'd remain immovably distant and irretrievably injured.

And that in spite of everything, she was going to marry him.

That she would, for any reason, was a miracle. That she carried his child was beyond imagining.

This cold, finite arrangement she'd made was still more than he'd dreamed he would have.

It was another chance.

Fourteen

"Have I told you lately how much I hate you?"

Laylah gazed at Aliyah, her cousin and that third precious al Shalaan female. Aliyah was scowling at her after wheeling a hanger teeming with wedding dresses for Laylah to try on.

Laylah sighed. "In the last hour? No."

The other women in the room chuckled. The wives of her cousins had all been recruited for the emergency wedding preparations. It was surreal to be home among so many women, with whom she had so much in common, from age to education to temperament.

There was one thing, however, she didn't share with them. They all had the unequivocal love of their men, and they all ranged from being ecstatically pregnant to delighted mothers many times over.

Johara, whom Laylah had helped prepare for her wedding to her cousin Shaheen almost three years ago, grinned. "Give it up, Aliyah. Every time we say we're never going to put together a royal wedding on short notice again, we end up with even less time in which to do it. Maybe next time we should say we'l do it in hours, and we'll end up with months on our hands?"

The women looked among themselves then snorted a col lective, *"Nah."*

Roxanne, Haidar's wife, chuckled. "Those men of ours en up crowding us for time no matter what we do."

Lujayn, Jalal's wife and the most recent bride, though sh had a two-year-old with Jalal, raised an eyebrow at Laylah "But for a change it was Laylah who squeezed us for time."

"Two days is not a squeeze," Aliyah lamented. "It's cruel.

Maram laughed. "Talk about leaving it to the last momen then wham." She gave Laylah a shrewd look. "Don't get m wrong, I'm all for making those impossible and impossib luscious men sweat it. It can only do their overriding sou good. But you *could* have given *us* some advance notice so w could restart preparations discretely while he stewed—as h needed to."

Laylah sighed, deciding to come clean. "I couldn't reall Strictly between us please, ladies, but the pink strip only ar peared yesterday."

Gasps of delight echoed around her room, followed by coo ing, if uncomfortable, congratulations. They could see sh wasn't happy about the pregnancy, that it made necessary marriage she didn't want.

All of the ladies had been in varied positions of relu tance during their weddings, too. But the problems and mi understandings in their relationships had been resolved. He wouldn't be.

From then on, the women did all they could to reinstate t cheerfulness of the proceedings and lift her spirits.

She cooperated, pretended interest as they talked color c ordination, bridal procession dresses and table trimmings. S kept up her pretense until they took her around the royal pala of Azmahar, deciding decorations.

Knowing this place, and the power it signified, was wh Rashid really wanted and not her was suffocating, literal and the world started to fade. Cries rang out in the dimness before everything turned to black.

Exiting a dark tunnel filled with sounds of distress, Laylah opened her eyes to see beautiful faces coated with concern.

She'd fainted. And the ladies had taken her back to her room.

"How are you feeling now, Laylah?" Maram asked, her voice soft and soothing as she continued to massage her hands.

Laylah tried to sit up, found Johara and Aliyah helping her. "I'm fine. Sorry for that."

"That first trimester can be a pain," Roxanne said, shuddering, no doubt remembering her own. "Good news is, you'll feel the best you ever did during the second one."

Not wanting to inform them her fainting spell had nothing to do with her pregnancy, she went along. "Can't wait."

"Wait until you see what we came back to the room to find!" Lujayn exclaimed as she rushed away.

Laylah's eyes widened as she saw what she came back holding.

Johara sighed. "You remember when Shaheen did this for me? Rashid, even though you're not ready to forgive him yet, is certainly as thoughtful and his choice is as perfect for you as Shaheen's was for me."

Laylah gaped at Rashid's "choice." A creation the likes of which she'd never imagined.

A one-piece Arabian/Indian masterpiece, it had a sleeveless bodice that nipped to a waist she was certain was the exact size of hers, with a décolleté that would emphasize her breasts and expose her neck and most of her shoulders and any necklace she would wear. With its base a golden mahogany the exact color of her hair and eyes, it was almost covered in breathtaking hand-embroidery of sequins, beads, pearls, crystals, semi-precious stones and appliqué, from the lightest coral to the deepest vermillion to the most vivid crimson, all intertwined with gold.

A skirt in hues echoing the top's embroidery cascaded in multiple layers of tulle and chiffon over a shimmering mahogany silk taffeta lining, its embellishments in the range of gold and russet, with ingenious scalloping at the hemline. A veil with heavily embellished borders was crimson where it would rest on her hair, gradually transforming to a luminescent golden-brown where it would trail on the floor.

But it was the patterns covering the whole outfit that robbed her of breath again. Those of Rashid's house.

It was as if he was…putting his *brand* on her with that dress, just like he had branded her body and soul.

The ladies interrupted her heavy-hearted musings, clamoring for her to try on the outfit at once. Just as she'd expected, it fit her perfectly. Rashid always knew exactly what he wanted, down to the last detail.

As Maram and Aliyah contacted their husbands to demand jewelry that would match the outfit, from Zohayd's and Judar's royal collections no less, Laylah watched the other ladies flipping through catalogues to pick their complementary dresses and wondered.

If she felt this terrible just preparing for this farce, how would she feel on the day itself?

The day was here. The *minute* she had to marry Rashid. And not really marry him.

The distinctive percussive music of her *zaffah*—her bridal procession—was already reverberating through the palace. Hundreds of voices were raised in the traditional congratulatory songs.

Aliyah and Maram were adorning her neck, arms and head in legendary jewels while Johara, Talia, Roxanne and Lujayn fussed with her veil, hairdo and makeup. They all looked stunning with their glowing beauty and bright spirits, their lithe bodies wrapped in sarilike dresses as exquisite as they were in reds and golds to complement her own gown.

She almost didn't recognize the splendid creature staring back at her in the mirror.

Rashid knew just how to package the royal acquisition he'd flaunt to the world tonight. The last piece in his master plan.

Her heavy-hearted musings halted as everyone rushed her out to lead her procession to the ballroom where the ceremonies were to be held. She hadn't seen any of the preparations as she'd been holed up in her quarters for the past two days. Now she felt she had entered a fantasy setting from Arabian Nights.

Brass lanterns and torches blazed everywhere, infusing the palace with a mystic ambiance. Every other decoration, from banners to veils to flowers, was color-coordinated with her gown and jewelry. Not that she could find any pleasure in her surroundings. Not when she couldn't forget why Rashid had "rented" the palace for their wedding. Not so that she could reclaim that part of her heritage, as he'd claimed, but so he could rehearse being its liege.

Even in her previous obliviousness, it had pained her knowing so much would be missing on this day—her mother there for her, her father giving her away. Now she knew her groom didn't really want to receive her, and this wedding was a charade, a sacrifice of her heart and dignity for the one thing that would mean more to her than her very life—her child…

Suddenly, her heartbeat drowned out the thundering music, and air, the world, disappeared.

Rashid stood alone at the wide-open gilded doors of the ballroom, shrouded in shadow even in the blazing illumination, as he'd absorbed all light.

In spite of herself, her starving senses rushed to devour his grandeur.

His outfit matched hers, only in darker, muted shades. Another detail he'd orchestrated to perfection. A mahogany *abaya* hugged his Herculean shoulders, adorned in embroidery echoing her gown's patterns, before cascading to his ankles like a cloak of enchantment. Underneath, burnt-sienna silk stretched across his formidable chest and abdomen, tucking into skin-tight same-color pants that gathered into darkest brown leather boots. A bronze metal belt hung around his powerful hips, anchoring a ceremonial dagger sheathed in a scabbard worked in bloodred and gold enamel.

This was a man whose legacy was rooted in fables, the embodiment of this harsh, magnificent land, a personification of its might and majesty, a shaper of the world around him.

He *was* born to be king.

If only he hadn't used her to claim his destiny.

If only he'd come clean. She would have done anything for him. Would have still had her heart and illusions intact.

But he hadn't. And she now only survived for their…*her* baby.

He stood there now, with those darkest-night eyes, searing her with his fake longing, his counterfeit entreaty.

"Laylah…"

The pure passion and anguish he made of her name nullified the din, quivered through her bones. How could it feel so real? How could she still want to throw herself into his arms?

Then those arms were coming around her. Feeling they'd singe her, she bolted. He let her stride ahead down the royal-red carpet that cut through the ballroom all the way to the *kooshah*. Intertwining gradations of red and gold chiffon veils undulated from Arabesque woodwork that embodied the gilded cage of matrimony, she guessed. He was beside her once more as she climbed a dozen crimson satin-covered steps to where they'd preside over the proceedings.

The *ma'zoon,* an imposing-looking cleric, was sitting in the middle of a pale gold sofa, with scrolls spread before him in triplicate. Haidar and Jalal flanked the sofa like bodyguards.

They would be *al shohood,* the witnesses of the marriage. She didn't know how Rashid had gotten them to consent to this, let alone to plead his case with her, when they'd been mortal enemies till recently. But she wouldn't put anything beyond his powers of manipulation. She'd refused her uncle's and cousins' offers to be her *wakeel,* her proxy. She wouldn't let them take a bigger part in this sham. She'd gotten herself into this, and she'd shoulder the sticky parts to the end alone.

As soon as they reached the platform, the music stopped. Almost plopping down beside the *ma'zoon,* desperate to look anywhere but at Rashid, her gaze swept the ballroom, where a hundred tables were set in the luxury level only someone of Rashid's means could attain. Around them sat a thousand of those who moved and shook the world. That was the kind of power Rashid wielded already. He probably wouldn't wield more as king.

Then he was leaning nearer behind the *ma'zoon.* She pre-empted him. "Shall we get this over with already?"

After failing to capture her gaze, Rashid exhaled, directed the *ma'zoon* to proceed.

After a while, he murmured, "*Habibati,* give me your hand."

Her gut wrenched. Her hand in his for the duration of the ritual was bad enough. But it was that *habibati* that scraped her nerves raw. Who was he still acting for?

She gave him a hand as stiff and cold as a corpse's, and tried not to flinch as that big, calloused hand that had taught her what passion and pleasure meant enfolded it. She kept her eyes fixed as he opposed their thumbs and the *ma'zoon* covered their hands in a pristine white handkerchief and placed his on top, then as she droned back the marriage vows the man recited.

After Rashid had, too, the *ma'zoon* addressed him, "Name your *mahr* and *mo'akh'khar al suddaag,* Sheikh Rashid."

The so-called "price of the bride," or as revisionists called it, the "bride's worth." That was paid in two installments. The *mahr,* at signing the contract, and the *mo'akh'khar,* "latter portion of the agreed-upon"—or in reality a severance payment—at termination of the marriage.

"My *mahr* is this." Rashid produced a box, gave it to her.

She took the scarlet velvet box, opened it.

A simple gold brooch lay against darkest red satin. Another rendering of his house's emblem. Very precise and delicate but by no means worth much in terms of cash value.

"It was my mother's." Rashid's voice numbed her with its fathomless magic. "It was my earliest memory. I was four when she told me it was my father's first gift to her. He was only eighteen when he bought it with his first pay. I slipped into her room the night she died. I kicked and screamed, but they wouldn't let me see her. All I could do was grab something of hers as they dragged me out of her room. It was this brooch. It is all I have left of her. It is the one possession I care about. Just as you are the one person, the one thing, I care about in this life."

"You…bastard."

The *ma'zoon* started at her viciousness.

Rashid's eyes only gentled. "Call me anything, think me a monster, but *arjooki ya roh galbi,* don't make it final. Leave the door ajar. Please, Laylah, take this."

When she only glared at him, her blood boiling, her heart splintering, he took out the brooch, and with trembling hands, he pinned it over her heart. It felt as if he'd pierced it.

Fighting the urge to rip it off and hurl it away, she didn't give him the satisfaction. At any emotional display, he'd only soothe her, appear as the loving, forbearing groom even more.

She glared at him as he signaled to Haidar and Jalal. "And my *mo'akh'khar* is this."

Haidar handed the *ma'zoon* a thick dossier. He opened it, read the first page before raising stupefied eyes to Rashid.

"Do I understand this correctly, Sheikh Rashid?"

Rashid nodded. "Yes. That is all my assets."

She gaped at him.

Then she finally asked, "What are you playing at now?"

"I never played at anything to start with, *ya habibati.* I am all yours, heart and soul. My assets are the least part of me."

"And I don't want them, like I don't want any part of you."

Rashid only exhaled, turned to the *ma'zoon.* "Document this."

The man did as asked, and an oppressive silence descended on them all. Then he invited her and Rashid to sign the three copies, and for Haidar and Jalal to stamp them with their seals.

On leaving the *kooshah,* the *ma'zoon* shot her a puzzled, disapproving glance. Haidar and Jalal gave her an entreating one. On Rashid's behalf. He *had* put them back in his pocket again.

The guests rose as one, toasted them with glasses filled with ruby-red *sharbaat ward,* rose-essence traditional wedding nectar.

As everyone resumed sitting, live Azmahrian music rose with their chatter, leaving bride and groom to their own conversation.

Talking with Rashid had once been all she'd wanted from life, something she'd reveled in and treasured until a few weeks ago. Now, she had nothing to say to him that wasn't bitter. She was done with bitterness. Which meant she wouldn't talk to him.

Suddenly she felt as if her left side had been set on fire. Rashid had slid across the sofa, almost touching her.

He met her cold glance with his soft and coaxing one. "You will have to talk to me at some point. Might as well start now."

She ignored him, pretended to wave to her *waseefat,* matrons of honor. They only shooed her away, urging her to respond to Rashid.

Fuming, she reached for her *sharbaat* and felt she'd touched a live wire. His hand. He'd beat her to the crystal glass.

When she wouldn't take it, he whispered, "Throw it in my face. I deserve far more for even considering my moronic plan."

Refusing to give him the outburst he was after, she took the glass, downed it, still not looking at him.

"Anger makes you thirsty? But this will only dehydrate you more. Also a sugar rush combined with adrenaline isn't advisable."

So. He'd given up the fiercely tender facade and was trying on the bedeviling one. She said nothing.

"That degree of self-control is admirable. I wonder—would it hold if I kissed you?" At her continued silence, he slipped an arm around her waist. "Shall we find out?"

Staring ahead, she said, "Being funny doesn't suit you."

"Talk to me, and I'll spare you my failed attempts at humor."

She flicked him a condescending glance. "You need your high-ranking guests to think we're having a great time? Afraid they'd realize your bride is sitting here under duress?"

"I care nothing about what anyone thinks. Test my claim."

"You're counting that I won't, so I won't upset my family."

His response got drowned out by the first part of the night's entertainment, an ingeniously choreographed and composed medley of beloved folk songs and dances.

As the guests were swept up in the energy of the performance, he pulled her closer. "Those songs are all for you."

She slid him a cool glance. "Thanks."

Tenderness filled his eyes again, poignancy, too. "Even if you say it's not real, I'm now your husband…"

"Only for a while, until the baby is born, max."

The indulgence in his eyes flooded her. "That's seven months from now. Remember what once happened in seven hours?"

"When I was a needy, self-deceiving twit? In vivid detail. What do you think the odds are of my falling for your manipulations again?"

"Beating impossible odds is what I do. I've triumphed over death many times. I'm going to conquer your aversion, even if it takes the rest of my life."

"It *will* take the rest of your life. Plus an hour."

His arm tightened around her. "Take the pound of flesh I owe you, *ya habibati*. Take as many pounds as you wish. Do it here and now." The feel of him against her, his consecutive blows of passion, entreaty and tenderness were chipping away at her control. "I dare you."

She pulled away as a storm of applause greeted the end of the performance, then rose to her feet.

Everyone turned to look at her as she came to stand at the edge of the *kooshah*. "Now to another time-honored tradition that no celebration in our region is complete without. Poetry."

A buzz rose. Her family consulted with each other if that was an arranged number.

"An ode to my new and loving groom," she started, perfect acoustics carrying her voice to the farthest corners of the ballroom.

"Howah kat'tamaseeh, yathreffod' dam'a enda muddgh fa-reesatuhu

Fahtaresu menhu i'tha arradto'l najjata

La ya'ghorannakom jamala mohayahu

Fama ajmal'l nomoor lakn korbuha ho'wal mammata."

(Like crocodiles he sheds tears when he gnaws his prey

So beware of him if you want to stay alive

Don't be fooled by the beauty of his visage

For how beautiful are tigers you'd never survive.)

Her quatrain was greeted by a shockwave of silence.

Suddenly a whistle pierced the hush, followed by a single pair of lazily clapping hands.

"Thank you, cousin. I was about to provoke an international incident to avoid watching another folklore number."

That was Amjad. Of course.

She couldn't pay him or anyone else attention. Rashid had gotten up to his feet, was approaching her like that stealthy predator she'd just likened him to.

He came to tower over her, his eyes the embodiment of adoration as he raised his voice. "An ode to the barren past when I could only look at my incomparable bride from afar:

Amorro ala'd dyari, dyari Laylah

Oqubbelo tha'l jeddara waa tha'l jeddari

Wama hobbo'l dyari shagafna qulbi,

Walaken hobbo man sakanna'd dyari."

(I pass by those dwellings, those of Laylah.

And I kiss these walls and those walls

It's not love of the place that has taken my heart

But of the One who dwelled in these halls.)

Silence again blanketed the vastness, raging inside her.

Instead of a defense, or an offense, he'd hit her with a quatrain from Qays Ibn Al Mulawah's poetry, the ancient poet renowned as *Majnun* Laylah, or Laylah's Madman.

And he'd used Qays's verses to claim he'd only loved and valued this palace and Zohayd's for her being in them.

Wow. Who would have thought he'd have poetry in his arsenal. But then as an ultimate tactician, he must have an infinite range of weapons. Seemed even now she hadn't realized the scope of his talent for subterfuge.

Before she could think of another unmasking verse, he went down before her on his knees. A collective gasp spread like wildfire around the ballroom. Everything inside her malfunctioned.

Looking exactly like the man she'd thought loved her with all his heart, he took her hands to his lips then, in a now ragged voice, recited the verses.

She gaped down at him long after he'd finished.

In lyrical Arabic, even more moving and exquisite than the famous verses, he'd said:

The bounty that you have given me, strip it not away
The generosity you have shown me, tear it not away
My ugly acts that you came to know, forgive them
I seek intercession from you with you
And I seek sanctuary in you from you
I come to you craving your beneficence
So act toward me with the mercy of which you are worthy
For I am not worthy of your vengeance.

She tried to breathe, failed yet again.

Had—had he just composed *that* on the spot?

He had insta-poetry among his powers of enthrallment?

"*Aaand* since nothing in this suddenly entertaining and memorable evening will top *that,* I suggest we eat."

Amjad again. And naturally, he had everyone following his lead, clapping a rising wave of approval at the unique verbal duel they'd witnessed between bride and groom.

Laylah tore her gaze from Rashid, still kneeling before her, bolted down the steps, and completed the evening's fireworks by running out of her own wedding.

She wanted to keep on running until she left everything behind, starting with her heart.

Running after Laylah had been out of the question. He'd already pushed too soon and had only driven her away further.

He'd followed her out of the ballroom, but not to pursue her. He left it to Haidar and Jalal to say whatever they pleased to the guests. He cared nothing about the guests continuing a wedding without the bride and groom when it seemed he was destined to continue his life without Laylah.

Night had deepened by the time he'd reached the seaside villa where she'd once told him she loved him, and which he'd bought for her, for them. He'd sell it in the morning. He couldn't stay here without her. And she wouldn't take it.

He walked across the veranda of the master bedroom suite to the balustrade, lost in thoughts as tumultuous as the sea. He…

"I've made a decision."

His every hair stood on end. *Laylah.*

He swung around to her, his heart thudding in disbelief. She was the last person he'd expected to see here, tonight, or ever.

She'd taken off the wedding gown he'd had made for her, and was in one of those flowing dresses she'd been wearing since they'd come back to the region. It looked as if it were weaved from moonlight. *She* was made of his every dream and was so…missed, he swayed where he stood with the sheer intensity of longing.

Her approach continued until she was flush against him.

His whole being, body and soul, surged at the feel of her. Confusion then hope were as overwhelming as his response. Was she…?

Her hand curled around his nape, brought his head down to hers. Before she took his lips in the kiss he'd been dying for, she ended all confusion. And hope.

She said, "Like you used me, took your pleasure when you felt nothing, I'll use you as cold-bloodedly, for my pleasure."

Fifteen

Her cold words doused the heat of her embrace.

He jerked back. "You can't mean that."

"I do." Her lips opened on his scar, what she'd turned into the trigger of his every uncontrollable desire. "You're fantastic in bed, and you are the man in my life—for now. I'll take my pleasure from you. As is my right."

He tried to hold her off, to hold back from snatching her. "You have every right to everything in me."

Her teeth nipped his chin. "I want nothing else from you."

"But I do. I want your love, your trust."

It was she who pulled away this time. "Sex is all I can give you. Ask for more, and I'll walk out, and you will see me only from afar until it's time to end the marriage."

It was in her face. She meant it.

If he said no, he'd lose her now, not later.

But if he said yes, he might still have a chance. He might still melt her in the inferno of their passion.

There was no choice really. A beggar had none.

Exhaling his defeat, he swept her up in his arms.

As soon as he put her down on the ground by the bed she charged him, climbed him, wrapped herself around him. His senses blazed with her hunger, his heart crumbled now she'd stormed out of it.

He tried to lower her to the bed, but she twisted in his arms, made him change direction, take her on top.

He watched her sweep off her loose dress, ablaze with exquisiteness, revealing another of those mind-messing creations he'd chosen for her in such intense pleasure and anticipation, the scarlet emphasizing the magic of her coloring and worshipping the perfections of her lushness. His hands trembled over her soft stomach where the miracle of their passion was growing, delight and dejection almost rupturing his heart.

Praying she'd reclaim him from the wasteland of her alienation, he opened himself to her possession, let her devour him and dominate him, drowning in her desire as she exposed him to its full measure, even as she withheld the spiritual part he needed most, was withering without. She ignited fever all over him until she claimed the manhood that been created to mesh them together, to give her pleasure.

Thrusting his hips to her ravenous rhythm, sinking deeper into her hunger, his hands shook all over her, his body and heart in her power. After a lifetime of sufficiency and restraint, his dependence on her was devastating, yet vital.

Her fingers dug into his buttocks, demanding his full surrender, what he'd learned to give her. His hand convulsed in her hair as his loins exploded, as she drained him, yet only left him crazed for more, for her.

He tried to snatch her up to his heart, but she took him over again, straddling him, her eyes as mindless as he felt with the need to merge. "I want you, Rashid."

"*Aih, ya hayati kollaha,* my whole life, want me." He helped her position him at her entrance. "Take all of me…"

She took him in one downward stroke.

A whiteout of sensation blinded him as her scorching core engulfed him, his home inside her. His only home.

Senses reignited when he'd forged all the way inside her, felt her shuddering all over him, inside and out, his name a litany of moans on her lips.

He knew how she felt, frenzied, as he rose with her impaled on him, leaned against the wall, spread her buttocks in his palms.

"Ride me, *ya rohi*. Take me and take your pleasure of me."

Hands bracing against his shoulders, thighs trembling, she slid up half his shaft when he engulfed one nipple in his mouth. Her hands slipped off his shoulders, had her crashing down on him, lodging him at her womb, her wail of stimulation tearing through both of them. "Rashid...do it..."

He obeyed, holding her hips and moving her up and down his length to the rhythm of his suckling and confessions. "Do you feel what you're doing to me? I never dreamed pleasure like this existed..."

Her fingers dug into his flesh, for breaching the sex-only stipulation. But he had to try to reconnect with her.

He rolled her around, slid up her moist, silken flesh, stretched her farther around his invasion, fighting to hold back the impending avalanche.

Throbbing in her depths, he rose above her. "Heaven would be nothing compared to being inside you." Her teeth sank in his scar, punishing him. His head pitched back on the excruciating pleasure. "*Aih*, Laylah, punish me and take me back—all of me."

At his plunge all the way into her, she shrieked, her inner muscles squeezing his length in a fit of release. He rode the breakers of her orgasm in a fury, surrendering to the pleasure he'd only ever known with her, jetting his essence into her milking depths, swearing his love as swell after swell of agonized completion swept him. "*Atawassal elaiki suddegeeni—ahebbek, a'ashagek*...I beg you believe me, I love you, worship you. I never loved anyone but you, never lied about this."

She went limp beneath him.

Unreasoning fears crashed on him. He might have been too aggressive, hurt her, the baby....

He tore himself from her clinging depths. "Laylah…"

Her eyes were open and empty. Dread overcame him, until she suddenly moved, removing herself from his frantic grip.

Her voice was as lifeless as her gaze. "I'm only serving my purpose to you. You're serving yours to me now, so it's a fair deal. But if you don't stop saying you love me, I will stop being with you at all."

Unable to look her rejection in the eyes anymore, he rose off the bed, needing to seek refuge anywhere but where she was.

Before he exited the room, he turned to her, announced his submission to her sentence. "I'll agree to anything you want."

What Laylah wanted amounted to hell on earth.

The next weeks set the pattern. She wouldn't let him into her life in any form. Not during the day. At night, she drew him back into the vortex of need. Even with her emotional coldness, their physical passion blazed out of control, scorching his body in satisfaction, and his soul in sorrow.

He'd reached the point where he knew. Though he'd take anything he could have of her at the price of his own destruction, he couldn't.

He'd soon be forced to end this.

"I'm now forced to make a decision."

Amjad sounded serious. For a second. Then he wiggled his eyebrows at Laylah, Haidar and Jalal where they sat side by side in his office. He'd summoned them urgently an hour ago and had refused to say anything until they were all there and sitting before him like an audience.

Amjad went on, "But then I'm the only one qualified to make one around this region."

Haidar, who sat beside Laylah with Jalal on her other side, huffed. "Spare us, Amjad."

"How can I? You can't live without my harassment." Amjad turned his smirk on her. "But I lied. I've long made my decision. It's in your court now, Laylah."

He wanted her to pass her verdict. On Rashid.

Though he'd made his, if she let her personal turmoil dictate an unfair one, he'd obey it.

It was up to her to deprive Rashid of becoming king.

But she'd never been vindictive this way, not even toward her worst enemy. And Rashid wasn't even… Was—was… Whatever he was, it had been heartache talking when she'd threatened that. Even at the height of her agony, even now as she felt her time with him ticking away, her belief in Rashid as the best king never wavered.

"Sorry, guys." She winced at Haidar and Jalal. "But I do believe he's the best man for the job."

"Our Aal Shalaan treasure has spoken." Amjad's sardonic smile grew dissecting. "So…is this your revenge? Pushing him onto the throne you believe he manipulated you to get, when you know you're only shoving him into a pit of thorns?"

Her lips trembled. "You seem to be quite comfy on yours."

"Only because I have Maram on my lap. Rashid no longer has you." So he knew how things remained between her and Rashid. Everyone probably did. Amjad's gaze bored into her. "Sitting on that throne without you will be agony without the ecstasy."

Her heart twisted. "Rashid is nothing like you. He doesn't need anyone."

Amjad huffed. "Did I ever look like I needed anyone? Turns out I do need one person. Maram. Like Rashid needs you."

How she wished that were true.

She rose before the tears that lurked a word away escaped. "I gave you my opinion. It's your decision now who to back."

Amjad had backed Rashid.

Haidar and Jalal, to Laylah's surprise yet again, endorsed his decision wholeheartedly.

Rashid would be king of Azmahar.

His *joloos,* sitting on the throne, was in two days.

This had been what he'd wanted so fiercely. What he deserved. What would he do now that he'd gotten it?

She was giving herself a nervous breakdown wondering when he walked into the suite in his house where he'd left her that first night, and every night since.

He never came to her this early. That, along with the intensity in his gaze, had hope suddenly surging inside her.

She found herself on her feet. He was her man, her soul, and even if he never loved her like she loved him, with all his passion, he must care as much as he was capable of. They would share a tough life, filled with duty and responsibility, but they'd make it if they had each other, and their baby...

Everything came to a stumbling halt as he caught her seeking hands. And the look in his eyes.

It was as if he was saying goodbye.

Then he said worse. "I wish it could have been different, but there's no use wishing. I can't...sleep with you anymore."

She'd thought her heart had been pulverized before. It hadn't been, or it had started to heal. He smashed it all over again. This time she knew there would be no putting it back together.

Agony suddenly poured from her. "You never 'slept' with me. The only time I woke up to find you still with me was that first night, and you only stayed to clinch your deal."

He said nothing. Just kept looking at her as if he, too, was devastated. It made her insane with pain.

"I have no doubt you'll do everything possible to claim the baby when it's born, but I demand my every right to it documented now, not then."

"Laylah..."

She spoke over him. "As for us, if you won't 'sleep' with me, then I have no use pretending this marriage is real. Our deal is over. I want a divorce. *Now.*"

He closed his eyes. Then before her heart could break on one more fractured beat, he turned and strode out.

Collapsing where she stood, she wept until she felt herself coming apart.

The moment he had what he wanted, he'd thrown her aside. Just like her mother had prophesized.

But he wouldn't do it yet. Not before he sat on that throne that meant everything to him.

Like she meant nothing.

The day of the *joloos* had come.

Rashid hadn't.

When Maram had said he hadn't come to the rehearsal ceremony, Laylah thought he'd show up at the last moment. He hadn't. Nobody knew where he was, or what had happened. According to everyone, he seemed to have disappeared off the face of the earth.

She was going out of her mind.

Something terrible must have happened. There was no other explanation for why he'd miss the most important day of his life. And if something had happened to him...

Another storm of weeping wrung her out as she prayed, again and again and again.

Let him be okay, let him fulfill his destiny. It doesn't matter that he doesn't love me. I love him. I always will...

"Laylah."

The deep voice hit her like a blow to the heart.

Because it wasn't Rashid's.

It was Haidar's. Jalal was with him.

She staggered around to them, her eyes and hands rabid as she clung to them, shook them. "Did you find him? Is he okay? *Tell me!*"

Haidar scowled down at her. "What do you care? Don't you hate him now?"

A huge sob tore out of her. "I—I could never hate him. I will always love him...no matter what..."

"That isn't what you've made him believe. He believes you hate him so absolutely, he's self-destructing in despair."

Horror mushroomed inside her. "You—you mean...?"

Jalal exhaled. "You need to sit down when we tell you this."

And she wailed. *"Laa...laa...ya Ullah...laa..."*

"He *hasn't* hurt himself." Haidar's assertion broke the rising wave of panic. It rose again as he exchanged a look with Jalal as if agreeing on divulging something terrible before pushing her down firmly on the sofa. "Though he swore us to secrecy, at peril of some creative retribution, you need to know everything."

As they sat down, her soul seeped down her cheeks with the terror of anticipation.

"You know why Rashid joined the army," Jalal started.

He'd joined to pay off his guardian's debts. The army in Azmahar had been offering top recruits lucrative salaries and educational opportunities. Rashid had calculated he'd repay those debts in five years, get a better education than the one he'd been able to afford, and become a soldier, a career he'd always admired.

Haidar and Jalal had tried to dissuade him. Hostilities had been brewing between Azmahar and Damhoor and they didn't want him joining the army in time to be sent to war. But he'd made up his mind. And war had broken out.

On one mission, his squad leader had led his troops astray in the desert. They would have perished if not for Rashid. Using what he'd learned alongside Haidar and Jalal in the harshest survival methods, he'd led his squad to safety. Laylah remembered those weeks when she'd nearly gone mad fearing for him. Zohayd and Judar had mediated peace. But that hadn't been the end. She'd continued to go insane with worry as he'd fought in more armed conflicts.

But Rashid had survived them all, done all he'd set out to do, obtained one degree and promotion after another. Then he'd disappeared.

Haidar continued as if reading her thoughts. "You remember when he seemed to disappear? He'd started working in intelligence. And he discovered the threads of our mothers' conspiracy."

Her heart, having expended all its force, flailed feebly as

she realized that the coming revelation would be worse than anything she'd imagined.

"He went undercover to get proof, told me he got a promotion and would be under the radar. Thinking he didn't want to see me again, I told him I didn't care if I never heard from him again."

A skewer twisted in her chest. How hurt Rashid must have been at the apparent lack of caring from his lifelong friend.

Jalal exhaled. "But though we *both* treated his choice like brats who only cared they couldn't have their friend around all the time, he was hoping that he was wrong about our mothers. Knowing what we do now, I'll bet he considered *you* more in his efforts to find proof *against* the conspiracy. Instead, he only found incontrovertible proof against our mothers. He still decided to give us a chance to do something about it first." Jalal dragged his hands down his face. "But on his way to see us, he was attacked and abducted."

She fell back in a nerveless mass. She'd been right. That first night *had* been like déjà vu for him.

Haidar carried on. "His kidnappers were our mothers' flunkies. They tortured him for the information he'd uncovered as well as for intel he had that our mothers' needed to perfect their plans. At one point, he managed to call me. He was in such bad shape I thought he was drunk. He told me where he thought he was, begged me to help. I rushed over, but found nothing at that address. It was another of our mothers' contingency tricks. They instructed his kidnappers to text me from that phone and apologize for calling me while drunk, before they destroyed it so that I couldn't trace it.

"Rashid thought I didn't come to his rescue because I, and Jalal, were in on the conspiracy. Even though he was almost broken in mind and body, that agonized him so much, he struck back. He killed his captors and crawled across Zohayd's desert to Damhoor's border. The injuries those monsters had carved in his body—which were sliced open every time they started to heal—were so badly infected, he almost died. After spending weeks between life and death, he was stabilized, but no surgery could fix the scars. And I think his psychic scars ran deeper.

"He couldn't do anything about the conspiracy, since he'd lost all the evidence. When our mothers were exposed, he thought *we'd* pretended to abort their conspiracy so we could plot another day. Meanwhile he'd become friends with King Malek of Damhoor, and using his IT knowledge and intelligence techniques, Rashid developed an impenetrable defense system for him. King Malek offered him a ministry, but Rashid preferred to take his payment in hard cash to start his own business. And to pursue what had become his major goal—punishing us, by 'assimilating our ill-earned achievements.' He said he considered this a worse injury than exposing us, but I believe he was still unable to hurt us *that* badly. He's far more mushy-hearted than any of us thought possible.

"Then the chain reaction happened in Azmahar, and he was pitted against us for the throne of what he considered *his* kingdom. He decided he would do anything rather than let either of us take it. The rest you know."

Agony too great to find physical manifestation cleaved into her soul.

Rashid...Rashid...all this time...

"There's more." Her gaze slid sluggishly to Jalal. How could there be more? "There's a reason he didn't make it to his *joloos*."

She'd forgotten about that. She wished she could forget who she was. The daughter of the woman who'd mutilated the one man she'd ever loved.

"He suffered from post-traumatic stress disorder. He'd said it was under control, but he called us just now to say it's back, making him unfit to be king. He told us to toss a coin to decide who will sit on the throne and who will be crown prince."

Jalal stopped, looking uneasily at Haidar.

There could be nothing worse than what they'd already shared.

Haidar let her know there was always worse. "He said he should have never come back, should have died in one of those wars or in the desert, that it would have saved everyone endless trouble. He also said he understands if you don't want him near his child and he'll abide by anything you decide."

Desperation drove her to her feet. *"Where is he?"*

Haidar's face twisted. "The place that means the most to him."

She jumped on that. "I heard he bought his old family home."

Jalal shook his head. "We thought that at first, but we realized that's not where he's been happiest."

"Then *where?*" she cried out.

Haidar exhaled. "His Chicago loft."

During the trip to Rashid's loft, Laylah sank deeper in despair. What if Haidar and Jalal were wrong about his whereabouts? What if they'd been right, but he'd already left? She couldn't dare believe their rationalization of why he'd go there. After all she and her family had put him through, how could he consider the place where they'd started their relationship to be the place where he'd been happiest?

She'd come alone. She couldn't bear for anyone to come with her to the one place *she'd* been her happiest. Where she'd been Rashid's. Before the world had intruded and almost destroyed everything.

A few steps into the vast loft had her battered nerves jangling. With that familiar pleasure that burned through them.

Rashid *was* here.

Then he materialized out of the darkness at the mezzanine.

After staring down at her for an eternity, he started down the stairs. "You didn't have to come. I'll grant you the divorce and anything else you ask for."

"I—I'm not…I'm here to…" She swallowed the jagged lump of agony in her throat. Then she blurted out, "They told me everything."

Harshness replaced the blankness on his face. "I will make them regret telling you."

"*You* should have told me."

"You should never have known any of this."

"I had a *right* to know. It's my *mother* who did this to you."

His face hardened more. "You had enough spoiling your memories and soiling your psyche where she is concerned. There was nothing to be gained if you knew more, and so much to be lost."

He'd been protecting her. When he should have used this to hit back at her, at least to defend himself.

"What she did to me were the misdemeanors of an overbearing mother who didn't know when to let her daughter breathe on her own. What she did to you was an unforgiveable *crime*."

The turbulence in his eyes ratcheted up. "And that's why I didn't want you to know. So you wouldn't feel like this. I never wanted to add this to your disillusions."

And she couldn't bear being away from him for one more second. "Rashid…"

He jerked away from her. "Don't. Don't touch me, don't even come near me. It's not safe. I'm not safe."

A sob hacked her chest. "*Ya Ullah ya,* Rashid…I'm so sorry…"

"Don't…" he gritted. "Don't pity me. Just don't."

She lunged at him, hugged him with all her strength even as he tried to push her away. "It's not pity…*ya Ullah*…it's rage and regret and pain so fierce it shreds my heart with every breath."

Trying to undo her frantic hold, he groaned, "No, Laylah. Don't feel bad about it. You had nothing to do with this."

She clung harder. "It's still my mother who did this to you."

His arms fell to his side, surrendering to her embrace. "It's in the past. Let it go. I have."

She raised her face, seeing him blurred through the tears. "It's very much in your present, in your future."

"I swear to you, it's not."

"I know about your PTSD," she sobbed.

His headshake was adamant. "Memories of that ordeal are no longer what's fueling my instability."

Tears slowed down. "What is then?"

His shrug was forced. It told her he was going to lie. Then he did. "I guess it's self-perpetuating now."

And she had to know. "Is that why you never slept with me?"

His nod was difficult. "It's why I don't have anything around me when I sleep. I used to wake up with things broken, with sheets shredded and mattresses gutted with the shards."

He'd been killing his abusers over and over in his nightmares.

"I couldn't risk lashing out at you as I wrestled with my demons, even when I thought I had my condition under control. Then it was no longer under control, and I even had episodes while awake. I can no longer be around you."

"If memories aren't why your PTSD flared, what is? Was it the stress of seeking the throne, the fear of losing it?"

He closed his eyes. When he opened them, he let her see all the way into him for the first time. "It was the stress of seeking *you,* of having you yet not having you, and the fear of losing even that much of you. And I managed to fulfill my fears. I literally became *Majnun* Laylah, making it imperative to inflict your loss on myself. But then I lost you irrevocably that day you discovered my original plans. I only kept telling myself I might get you back. It was when I faced that I never would that my PTSD crashed back a hundredfold. You were the one who started me on the path to true healing and losing you has plunged me into worse than my worst days.

"I thought everything inside me was long dead. But you resurrected it all, made me discover hopes, emotions and needs I never knew I had. I suddenly found myself dependent on another human being. It was glorious, yet scarier than any mortal danger I had ever been exposed to. Then—everything went to hell. Knowing I'd lost your respect, your love, that I had broken your faith and your heart, being unable to heal you, is something I can never heal from."

And she charged him, deluging him in tears and kisses and pledges. "You never lost me or my love. You never will as long as I'm still alive, since that's all I am—love, for you. I was stupid and hurt and trying to protect myself. But I made that deal with you so I would still be with you, in hope that you'd love me someday, if only a fraction as much I love you. I've loved you forever, *will* love you forever." She pulled away to look into his eyes, her heart twisting. "But how can *you* love me, after what my family, after what *I* did to you? You *should* hate me."

He suddenly sank with her in front of the extinguished fireplace where they'd shared such ecstasies, his face trembling, his eyes filling. "You did far less than what I deserved. And your family made up for everything they'd ever done by having you. I might even love them for it."

A laugh of incredulity burst through the upheaval. "Now don't go overboard. But whatever you do, *I* will never forgive them."

He held her face between those callused hands that embodied tenderness and cherishing. "I need you to believe that one touch, one smile, one moment with you *has* atoned for all their crimes, has healed all my injuries. All I want now is for you to forget this and be at peace. If I have you, I have everything, past, present and future. I want only to be your lover and husband and father of our child."

"And king of Azmahar," she blurted out.

"Azmahar deserves someone unscarred inside and out."

"Azmahar needs *you.* And it's your destiny to rule the kingdom you defended and almost died for, the kingdom you've taken back from the brink of destruction and will now lead to prosperity. And that kingdom chose you. Like I did. Because you *are* the absolute best. Even your rivals think that. Hell, even Amjad thinks that. You *must* take your throne."

"On my life and honor, I will do anything you ever demand. But why not wait and see if I am the best choice for Azmahar?"

As she started to launch into another argument, he kissed her, silenced everything but the need to merge with him.

Not knowing how, she found herself where he'd first made her his as he came on top of her on the mattress she'd made him return after she'd found it far superior to any bed.

The next forever was consumed in finding their way back to each other, body, heart and soul.

What felt like a lifetime of bliss later, he moved her sweat- and pleasure-drenched body on top of his, caressed her all over, paying special attention to the belly that was starting to round.

"About the throne…" she began.

He cut her off. "About the honeymoon we never had. How about you tell me where you want to have it?"

She dove deeper into his embrace. "Right here. But…"

"There are too many reasons not to think of the throne now."

"Your PTSD flared up on my account. It should subside now."

"Even if it does, I can't be king. I need to be with you through your pregnancy and during our baby's birth and first months. I *will* make up for both of our lifetimes of alienation."

She ran adoring hands and eyes down his beloved face. "*Then* you'll consider taking the throne?"

"How about we take this one day at a time?" He gave her back the words she'd given him in what felt like another life. "Let's just savor this. What's the rush?"

"Uh…a kingdom with no king?"

He waved it away. "Haidar and Jalal will hold down the fort. It's good training in case one of them ends up on the throne."

As she opened her mouth, everything inside her stopped. At a sight she'd thought she'd never see.

Rashid's first full smile.

"How's that?" He tickled her out of her swooning. "Am I doing it right?"

She melted even more. "If I thought your scowl heart-stopping, your smile is possibly life-threatening."

And he treated her to another first, his unbridled guffaw.

"Ahh…" She lost all cohesion. "I'm gonna die!"

Still exposing her to the incomparable beauty of his grin, he countered, "You're gonna live. To love me and be loved by me."

Joy inundated her, that true ease finally entered his heart and made his smile ready and laughter possible.

Deciding not to push for the throne for now, she grinned widely back. "All I ever wanted is to be yours, and for you to be mine."

He illuminated her whole world and being with his delight and devotion. "Done. And done."

Epilogue

Haidar and Jalal scowled at Rashid.

He only raised serene eyes to them, grinning, delighted at how that still fazed them.

Haidar blinked, as if to clear his eyes from a burst of light and bit off the words, "You said a couple of months."

"And when was *six* months ever 'a couple'?" Jalal added, folding his arms over his chest, looking as unsettled at seeing him smile.

"You were both once intent on taking on the job permanently. What's so difficult about doing so for half a year?"

Haidar huffed. "Since you landed the bid, we rearranged our lives accordingly, and you ran and left us holding the baby."

He shrugged. "I did so *I* can hold my and Laylah's baby. And I'm not holding anything else until I do."

"Just give us a straight answer, damn you," Haidar growled before sitting next to him, grabbing his shoulder, looking deeply into his eyes. "Are you really okay now?"

"Far better than you can imagine." Rashid smiled at him, an act that came so easily to him now. "I have my own mind acle. And she's providing me with another one…in about a week's time."

Jalal sat on his other side. "*Then* we can be allowed to have a piece of you? You can be a husband, a father and a friend, too, you know. We've tried it and it works."

Rashid grinned at him. "If I don't expire of happiness when our baby boy is born, I'll squeeze you, and the throne, onto my list of priorities."

Haidar rolled his eyes. "Once we could never get you to crack a joke, now you're almost rivaling Amjad, your biggest fan and our biggest pain in the ass, in being irreverent. Laylah isn't a miracle worker, she's a saboteur."

"You found out my true agenda!"

As Haidar and Jalal turned whimsical gazes to their ribbing cousin, Rashid filled his sight with Laylah as she waddled down the stairs of their loft. She became more beautiful with every passing day.

Firelight beamed off the brooch she almost always wore. His *mahr*. What he considered his mother's gift to her.

He had another gift for her now. One from *her* mother.

He rose, looking at Haidar and Jalal. "It's a good thing you're here to hear this. I just learned this moments before you barged in." His arms went around Laylah, the one being who encompassed the world to him. "I've been reinvestigating this ever since you came back to me. And today I made sure. Your mother had nothing to do with my kidnapping."

Tears surged into her eyes as her whole face trembled. "You're not just—just…"

"I only ever hid things I thought were no longer relevant, but I never and will never lie to you, *ya mashoogati*. It's the truth. You can have your mother back now."

He received an armful of sobbing love and thankfulness in utmost gratitude, before he turned to Haidar and Jalal.

"I'm sorry, *ya shabaab,* but your mother was solely responsible for this." At their pained, resigned looks, he added, "But she didn't order my mutilation, or death, after they extracted the information. Her orders were to get the information without damaging me, then keep me prisoner until she carried out her plan. What they did was their own payback to me. I'd been responsible for their imprisonment or that of their relatives."

Haidar frowned. "Are you saying this to make us feel better?"

"With Sondoss as your mother, I doubt that's possible." At their grimaces, he grinned, making them do a hilarious double take. "Seriously, she's not as bad as I thought she was. She has lines she won't cross, which makes her dangerous and misguided but not a hardened criminal. As far as I'm concerned this—" he indicated his scar "—isn't her doing. So I basically forgive her. And so should you."

Haidar groaned. "It's a miracle we're so well-adjusted."

Jalal's eyes widened. "You're talking about us?" He shook his head as he rose, put his hand on Rashid's shoulder. "The only reason we're not as dangerous as our mother is because we found you so early on. And before we strayed too much after you left us, we found Roxanne and Lujayn."

Haidar rose, huffed a mirthless laugh. "That *was* a couple more catastrophes averted, thanks to the right people at the right time. So…" He placed a hand on Rashid's other shoulder. "Right *man,* when will you take your kingdom off our hands?"

"Uh…never?" As they all exploded in protests, he smirked. "I meant it's never going to be totally off your hands. Even after I take the throne, you'll share it with me. You pick your titles."

Jalal shook him in mock panic. "Please, not heir and spare. Harres and Shaheen suffer untold horrors being Amjad's."

"My heir is right here." He lovingly caressed Laylah's round belly, soaked up her adoration. "You can be anything and everything else."

"*Sokrunn ya rubb*—thank God!" Haidar pretended relief. "But we'll have to get back to you on that, *after* Roxanne and Lujayn tell us exactly what we'll be, and what we'll do."

Rashid laughed. "A very wise if terminally annoying king

once told me that a man can't call himself that until a woman has him totally whipped."

Haidar guffawed. "We're the manliest men who ever lived then."

Rashid looked down at Laylah, loving her, thanking the fates for her with every heartbeat. "*No* one is manlier than me."

A contest of anecdotes proving who was manlier followed, after which they settled everything else.

When he returned from seeing Haidar and Jalal off, he came down on the floor beside Laylah as she stretched on the couch, rubbing and kissing her belly soothingly.

Sighing her pleasure, she drew her hands luxuriantly through the hair that now brushed his neck. "Thank you, *ya rohi.*"

"I'm the one who's thankful I could give you this."

"I'm not only thanking you for doing all this in the hope of exonerating my mother of the one crime I would have never forgiven her for, or for giving me the chance to rebuild my relationship with her. I'm thanking you for being you, for being mine."

"You thank me for that every day. You spoil me."

"Tough. I will keep on thanking you. But then you do the same. Now give me the straight answer you didn't give the guys."

"I *am* doing a lot for Azmahar from here. But I will only go back there with our whole family accounted for. Whether to be king or not remains to be seen. This is the destiny I care about—being yours, and our baby's."

"The throne is the other half of your destiny!" She pulled him up to her by his hair. "Didn't you claim to be the 'manliest' man there is? Prove it. Say it is and that you'll take it."

Taking her lips, taking her into his arms and heart, he smiled his pledge. "*Amrek, ya habibati.* As you command, my love. It is, and I will."

Laughing delightedly, she enfolded him back in her arms and heart. "Good man."

* * * * *

REQUEST YOUR FREE BOOKS!

2 FREE NOVELS PLUS 2 FREE GIFTS!

♦ Harlequin® *Desire*

ALWAYS POWERFUL, PASSIONATE AND PROVOCATIVE

YES! Please send me 2 FREE Harlequin Desire® novels and my 2 FREE gifts (gifts are worth about $10). After receiving them, if I don't wish to receive any more books, I can return the shipping statement marked "cancel." If I don't cancel, I will receive 6 brand-new novels every month and be billed just $4.30 per book in the U.S. or $4.99 per book in Canada. That's a saving of at least 14% off the cover price! It's quite a bargain! Shipping and handling is just 50¢ per book in the U.S. and 75¢ per book in Canada.* I understand that accepting the 2 free books and gifts places me under no obligation to buy anything. I can always return a shipment and cancel at any time. Even if I never buy another book, the two free books and gifts are mine to keep forever.

225/326 HDN FEF3

Name	(PLEASE PRINT)

Address	Apt. #

City	State/Prov.	Zip/Postal Code

Signature (if under 18, a parent or guardian must sign)

Mail to the **Reader Service:**
IN U.S.A.: P.O. Box 1867, Buffalo, NY 14240-1867
IN CANADA: P.O. Box 609, Fort Erie, Ontario L2A 5X3

Not valid for current subscribers to Harlequin Desire books.

Want to try two free books from another line?
Call 1-800-873-8635 or visit www.ReaderService.com.

* Terms and prices subject to change without notice. Prices do not include applicable taxes. Sales tax applicable in N.Y. Canadian residents will be charged applicable taxes. Offer not valid in Quebec. This offer is limited to one order per household. All orders subject to credit approval. Credit or debit balances in a customer's account(s) may be offset by any other outstanding balance owed by or to the customer. Please allow 4 to 6 weeks for delivery. Offer available while quantities last.

Your Privacy—The Reader Service is committed to protecting your privacy. Our Privacy Policy is available online at www.ReaderService.com or upon request from the Reader Service.

We make a portion of our mailing list available to reputable third parties that offer products we believe may interest you. If you prefer that we not exchange your name with third parties, or if you wish to clarify or modify your communication preferences, please visit us at www.ReaderService.com/consumerschoice or write to us at Reader Service Preference Service, P.O. Box 9062, Buffalo, NY 14269. Include your complete name and address.

Bestselling Blaze author Jo Leigh
delivers a sizzling *The Wrong Bed* story with

Lying in Bed

Ryan woke to the bed dipping. For a few seconds, his adrenaline spiked until he remembered where he was. He groaned at the bright red numbers on the clock. "One a.m.? What…?"

The rest of the question got lost in the dark, but it didn't matter, because Jeannie didn't answer. His fellow agent on this sting must be exhausted after arriving late. "You okay?"

She tugged sharply on the covers, pulling more of them to her side of the bed.

Ryan could just make out her head on the pillow, her back to him, hunched and tight. Must have gotten stuck at the airport….

He curled onto his side, hoping to find the dream she'd interrupted. It had been nice. Smelled nice. He sighed as he let himself slip deeper and deeper into sleep…. The scent came back, a little like the beach and jasmine, low-key and sexy—

His eyes flew open. His heart thudded as his pulse raced. No need to panic. That was Jeannie next to him. Who else would it be?

Undercover jitters. It happened. Not to him, but he'd heard tales. Moving slowly, Ryan twisted until he could see his bed partner.

He swallowed as his gaze went to the back of Jeannie's head. Was it the moonlight? Jeannie's blond hair looked darker. And longer. He moved closer, took a deep breath.

"What the—" Ryan sat up so fast the whole bed shook. His hand flailed in his search for the light switch.

It wasn't Jeannie next to him. Jeannie smelled like baby powder and bananas. The woman next to him smelled exactly like…

She groaned, and as she turned over, he whispered, "No, no, no, no."

Special Agent Angie Wolf glared back at him with red-rimmed eyes.

"Jeannie is being held over in court," she snapped. "I'd rather not be here, but we don't have much choice if we want to salvage the operation."

She punched the pillow, looked once more in his direction and said, "Oh, and if you wake me before eight, I'll kill you with my bare hands," then pulled the covers over her head.

No way could Ryan pretend to be married to Angie Wolf. This operation was possible because Jeannie and he were buddies. Hell, he was pals with her husband and played with her kids.

Angie Wolf was another story. She was hot, for one thing. Hot as in smokin' hot. Tall, curvy and those legs…

God, just a few hours ago, he'd been laughing about the Intimate at Last brochure. Body work. Couples massages. *Delightful homeplay assignments.* How was this supposed to work now?

Ryan stared into the darkness. Angie Wolf was going to be his wife. For a week. Holy hell.

Pick up LYING IN BED by Jo Leigh.
On sale December 18, 2012, from Harlequin Blaze.

HBEXP1212JLREV